THE
Heart Breaker

USA TODAY BESTSELLING AUTHOR
RENEE HARLESS

Paperback Edition

Cover photo by Shutterstock and Pexels

Cover design by Porcelain Paper Designs

THE
Heart Breaker

USA TODAY BESTSELLING AUTHOR
RENEE HARLESS

M Y FINGERS ARE SHAKING AS THEY
hover over the shutter button of my phone
camera. The voice in the back of my head
keeps chirping, telling me that this is a bad idea, but my
resolve is strong. Closing my eyes, I take a deep breath
and then open them to gaze seductively into the full-
length mirror on the back of my closet door. I have no
idea what I'm doing, how I should stand or where to
place my hand, but I take the picture anyway, and before
I lose my confidence, I attach it to a message to my
boyfriend and click send.

I'm a good girl, the one you see walking down a
pathway with my nose in a book, setting my own
curfews, and never missing a class. But, it is my final year
of college, and I wanted to take a moment to step out of

my box. Be the girl that men fantasize about, like my roommate Sofie.

Sofie and I are opposites in every way; her hair is long, flowing and blonde, where mine is straight and brown. She has a sun-kissed tan year round, where I struggle with the fine line between pale and ghostlike. And her athletic body comes naturally, whereas mine comes from spending time at the gym to keep my curves in line. But regardless of our differences, we are best friends and have been since we met at college orientation four years ago.

A knock on my door sounds and I turn quickly still clutching my phone to my chest as Sofie strolls into my room as if she owns the place.

"Sofie!" I shout as I try to reach for something to cover up my naked body, but I come up empty-handed.

"What? It's not like I haven't seen a naked body before," she casually points out as she takes a seat on my bed while I reach into my closet to grab my bathrobe hanging on the other side of the door.

"Yeah, well not mine."

"Which is a shame, Blake. Your body is banging. I tell you that all the time." I huff at her as I tighten the band around my waist a bit too harshly to hold my robe in place. "So, did you do it?"

The nude selfie had been Sofie's idea. Last night, after drinking a few margaritas, I had confessed to her how my boyfriend, David, and I had been going through a rough patch. David and I have been together since freshman year, but recently, since he took over as President of his fraternity, he has been distant. I wanted to believe Sofie, that he was just busy and needed a quick reminder of what he was missing out on by dedicating himself to his fraternity, but I thought it was more than that.

When I first met David, I had been sitting by the fountain in the center of our campus waiting to meet my partner in the mentor program. The marketing department always paired two new students with one of their graduate students as part of a mentorship program to help them grow contacts in the field.

I had been waiting ten minutes past the time we were supposed to meet and just as I was about to leave, David, wearing his school baseball uniform, took the seat next to me and introduced himself. A few minutes later a boy walked up and bumped fists with David before turning his attention to me. I had recognized him from my classes. He was tall, with dark hair that fell just over his forehead and green eyes that shined in the sun. His baseball uniform matched David's, and when he turned to me, he introduced himself as Zack, my new partner.

I had pulled my attention away from Zack and watched as David stood up from the bench, but I could feel the newcomer's eyes still burning my skin. David had asked to take me to dinner that night and I agreed, excited to go on my first date. I remember hearing a growling sound from around us, but my excitement drowned it out as David reached out and typed my number into his phone.

As he left, I expected to begin my first project with Zack, but when I broke free from the trance David had put me in Zack was nowhere to be seen.

After our first date, David quickly staked his claim on me and we began dating exclusively, and though we worked through a few rumors of his playboy ways, we persevered and ignored them. Because I loved and trusted him. I was also certain that his best friend, Zack, was behind many of the rumors. Besides the few projects we worked on together, Zack always steered clear of being around David and me unless he had one of his many female fans on his arm. He hated me, though I was never quite sure why. David always claimed it was because he was jealous that I held the highest grades in my department but I wasn't sure that was the reason.

"Did you?" Sofie repeats, breaking me free from reminiscing about better times. The times when I didn't believe I had seen David with his arm draped over the shoulders of another girl; a girl I believe texted him from an unknown number.

"I did."

"You go, girl!" she cheers as she bounces on my bed clapping her hands enthusiastically. "So, what did he say in response?"

I peer down at the phone still in my hand and shrug when I don't find any incoming texts. My gaze drifts back to Sofie whose smile tilts downward.

"He'll like it, right?"

Sofie bounds from the bed and wraps her arms around my body. "Sweetie, what's not to like? Hell, I'd like it. I'm sure he just hasn't had a chance to check it yet. Why don't we watch a few episodes of Friends and order some Chinese?"

"Okay. That sounds good. I have to work early tomorrow so I don't want to be up too late."

Chuckling, Sofie says as she heads toward our small apartment kitchen, "You're never up late, Blake. Do you even know what the world looks like past eleven?"

My body rocks against the mattress of my bed as an intruder nudges my shoulder. I peak my eyes open and notice that my room is still dark, the sun just beginning to make itself known through my window.

"Blake," Sofie whispers more sternly with another nudge, and I finally turn over in bed to look at her.

Stretching my arms above my head, I ask, "Hey, what's up?"

"I'm so sorry. So so sorry."

Sofie never apologizes for anything, so to see the anguish on her face, I know that something terrible has happened.

"What's going on?"

Silently she hands me her phone and I see a message pulled up with my nude selfie in the response box asking if it was me.

"Who is that?" I whisper, staring down at the phone in horror.

"That's Jamie, one of the members of David's frat."

"How did he. . ." I trail off, finally tearing my eyes away from the device held tightly in my grasp.

"The picture was sent to the entire fraternity. Every member in their group message, including the pledges."

"Why would. . ." I begin to ask but the sob I'm working to hold back breaks free.

Sofie reaches over and holds me against her body as I unleash my despair at experiencing every young woman's fear of having their private photos exposed.

"We need to go talk to David. Maybe there is an explanation."

Suddenly, as if a switch has been flicked, a spark of anger wells up deep inside of me.

"An explanation? What kind of explanation is there?"

"Well, I don't know. But I'm going with you," she says as I bound off the bed and throw on a pair of jeans and a long-sleeve shirt.

"You don't have to." My emotions are battling between sadness, embarrassment, and anger as I grab my car keys off my desk and make my way to the front of the apartment, slipping my feet into a pair of sandals beside the door.

"Oh, you can bet your ass I'm coming. No one does this to my friend even if it was an accident. Fucking asshole," Sofie murmurs as she picks up her pace to follow me to my car. "Let's go."

The fraternity house that David lives in with Zack and about ten other guys is completely dark when we pull up. I don't hesitate as I exit the car and begin to make my way to the back of the house knowing that they keep the door unlocked for any brothers coming and going late at night. Luckily, the college is just on the outskirts of the small city so crime is low and they've never had to worry about a break-in. Until today. Until my boyfriend has single-handedly tried to ruin my life and reputation.

Sofie follows closely behind as I step into the kitchen at the back of the house and make my way toward the staircase leading to the second floor where David's bedroom is located. I haphazardly kick a few empty beer cans, not caring if the noise wakes any of the brothers. I'm too hot right now to care about any of their reactions.

Just as we step onto the upper floor landing, Zack steps out of the steaming bathroom wearing a white towel around his waist and nothing else. If I wasn't so consumed in the hatred sprinting through my veins, I might have taken a second to admire the water droplets as they drift down his muscled chest.

Just as surprised to see me as I am him, he stops walking and pauses to greet us.

"Hey Blake, Sofie, what are y'all doing here?" he asks casually as if he hadn't just seen me naked. I'm actually surprised to see that his eyes never stray below my face to see if the goods match the picture.

"Is he in there?" I spew as I point toward David's closed bedroom door.

"Well, yeah, but, Blake, you may not. . ." he starts, but I don't finish listening as I spring forward and turn the knob to the door and swing it forcefully. The door opens with such flourish that it bangs against the wall with a clatter, startling the two people lying in David's bed. The two naked people in David's bed, one of which is my boyfriend.

"Blake!" David shouts and tries to wrap himself in his sheet, but he isn't able to pull it away from the blonde woman sharing his bed. "It's not. . ."

". . .what it looks like? What a joke." Stomping into the room, I flick on the overhead light watching as the two people grimace under the brightness. "How could you do this to me, David? Why would you embarrass me like this?"

He squirms a bit under my gaze but tries to look as if he didn't do anything wrong. The look is not convincing. "I'm sorry, baby. We were drinking and Candace and I were being stupid. It meant nothing."

"I'm not talking about the cheating, dammit!" I shout loud enough to echo in the house. I can hear a few of his fraternity brothers waking up and moving around. "Why would you send that picture of me to everyone? What would possess you to do that?"

"I didn't. . .it was an accident. . .I mean, I lost my phone last night," David tries to explain, but I just grab the lamp on his nightstand and chuck it across the room.

"I hate you!" I scream at the top of my lungs before I feel a pair of arms wrap around my shoulders pulling me out of the room.

"Come on," Sofie whispers in my ear as I start to come back into myself. My body shakes and the wetness of my tears feels cold against my cheeks.

Just as I step back into the hallway, I hear David cry out, "It was Zack. He tricked me into sleeping with Candace, telling her that this was his room and then he stole my phone."

I'm not sure what possesses me to believe him, maybe it's the fact that I've hated Zack from the very moment we met despite how my skin prickles whenever he's near, but I do. And when I watch Zack step out of his room carrying David's phone, I walk up to him feeling every ounce of hate bleeding from my veins and land a right hook onto his chiseled jawline. I can hear the crunch of my knuckles, and it hurts like a bitch, but I'm thankful that I take a boxing class offered at the gym because his jaw probably hurts more than my hand.

"What the fuck, Blake?" he barks as he cradles his chin.

Leaning forward, I bring my face within inches of his.

"I hate you. I hate you more than anything in this world," I tell him and my voice breaks at the end causing Sofie to tug me back down the stairs.

"What the fuck did you tell her?" I vaguely hear Zack scream at David, but I don't stay to hear anymore. I tuck myself into Sofie and pray that I can make it through another eight weeks and walk across the stage so that I never have to see any of these people again. The people that in the course of twelve hours have destroyed any faith that I have in men.

I packed up my last bag before stowing it inside the trunk of my tiny sedan. I've finally graduated from college. After all of the drama that unfolded only a fistful of weeks before, I took a couple of days to wallow in self-pity, then realized that I was letting him win. I was letting my douche of an ex destroy everything that I have been working so hard to accomplish. The first time I saw him around campus I made sure to tell him exactly how I felt about everything he's put me through. I said my piece and then turned around and walked away, not wanting to let him have the final word.

"That's the last one," I tell Sofie, who is standing beside her father's luxury SUV waiting for his right-hand man to carry down all of her belongings. "You'll make sure to call and text me every day, right?"

"Without a doubt, bestie," Sofie replies as she wraps her lithe arms around my shoulders, holding me tight. Sofie has been my savior since the rug was pulled out from underneath me. She was my confidante and encourager.

Pulling away she asks for the fifth time today, "So you're ready to start your internship at Brecken Marketing?"

"Absolutely. I want to learn from the best and hopefully land a job there after the internship."

"You'll do it. You're amazing at everything you put your mind to. Oh, here is Daddy and Sven; time for me to go. I'll call you later. Let me know when you're all settled."

"Will do. I love you, Sof."

With one last embrace, Sofie returns my sentiment and heads on her way. I send a message to my father, who was unable to get away from work for longer than to watch me walk across the stage, and let him know that I was beginning my trek to Atlanta.

With a deep inhale of the fresh mountain air, I get into my car and turn toward the highway. My moment to rise and conquer is truly beginning. I have no plans to stay the same timid wallflower I had always been. I had dreams – big ones. And no one is going to stand in my way.

Six Years Later

S HUFFLING DOWN THE HALLWAY, I PLOP
the oversized box in my arms onto the makeshift
desk in my new office. I use the word office
loosely since this is really the old garage attached to my
dad's house that he had sealed up and overhauled into a
working space for me.

"Is that the last of them?"

I turn around to find Sofie with her laptop in her
hands as she walks through the side door and turns
around in the finished space.

"Yep. So, what do you think?"

Sofie finally makes eye contact with me, and I can
see that she is debating on telling me what I want to hear
or the truth. The situation I've put us in is catastrophic.

"Just tell me, Sofie."

Sliding her bag from her shoulder, she sets it and her laptop onto the desk before walking toward me. She gently places her hands on my shoulders as she says, "I think that you're doing a remarkable thing by helping out your dad. And I'm thrilled that you're going to let me work with you. I would have been happy working out of your old bedroom, Blake. You know that."

"But?"

"But I'm afraid you're going to run yourself ragged. We have a few accounts that you were able to pick up locally, and they're doing great, but is it enough? I just don't want to see you struggle at something you're so good at."

I hear her, every word, every fear that has been hounding me these past six months as I try to sort my life and mingle it back with my father's. I had been working at a top-notch marketing firm in Atlanta when I got the call that my father had been in a life-changing work accident. An accident that not only changed his life, but mine too. He and my mother separated not long after I was born and my father maintained primary custody after their divorce. Since neither of us has heard from my mother since the day they separated, I was all he had.

After taking an emergency leave of absence, I came home to find my father in a coma with little to no use of his extremities. The next three months were touch and go as my father's body worked to heal itself and I returned to work, waiting patiently to hear that my father had pulled through. Then the medical bills started rolling in. I used what little savings I had to pay what his insurance wouldn't cover while we fought with his workers' compensation to reimburse the payments.

Just when things started looking up, my father took a turn for the worse as an infection wreaked havoc on his body and the hospital called to tell me to find someone that could take care of my father during the day while he worked to rehabilitate his body. The doctor thought a year or two would be the best prognosis for his recovery, but my father would never be able to return to work. His ability to walk was the therapist's goal, but until he reached that milestone, he would be confined to a wheelchair, possibly for life.

My boss was understanding and allowed me to finish the remainder of my projects from our small town of Hollisville in Virginia just outside of Charlottesville, but once the projects reached completion, I was let go.

With no money, no job prospects, and dad's meager disability payments I decided to use the remainder of my small savings and start my own marketing firm. The small town rallied around me and gave me business where they could. I hated being a charity case, but I couldn't look a gift horse in the mouth.

Amazing recommendations from my previous employer landed me a small athletic clothing company's contract and they have been thrilled with my work thus far. Unfortunately, my profits aren't enough to pull my father out of the financial hole that we seem to be drowning in.

Being my best friend, I asked Sofie if she would consider moving to Hollisville and working with me, using the business degree she happened to graduate with to help manage the small company. Of course, Sofie being Sofie, she didn't even bat one of her glued-on eyelashes and she left her socialite lifestyle in New York behind and showed up the next day.

I had turned down her offer to invest in the business, not wanting to feel as if I owe anybody anything. My father did the same when she offered to help pay his bills. He was firm that he would fight against his employer to get his fair share of workers' compensation. The lawyer we hired was eating up all of our extra funds so I've since taken all correspondence into my own hands.

Turning my fake smile toward Sofie, I flash my pearly whites at her. "Everything will be fine, because it will all work out the way it was meant to. I have to believe that."

"And I believe in you. That's why I'm here. And, on my way in I got word that Fleming Coffee has accepted our contract request."

"Really?" My voice raises an octave as I shout joyfully.

"Yes, but there is a catch," Sofie adds, immediately diminishing my happiness.

"What kind of catch?"

"Well, it seems that they are entertaining a few different companies. Some big, some small. Each of the heads of the company have their favorites." Sofie stops when she takes a look at my face, lips pinched together and brows furrowed as if I'm snarling. "What is it?"

"Don't you know who runs Fleming Coffee?" I ask her. The coffee chain is a staple along the east coast, and word is that they're hoping to expand nationwide. The contract is lucrative so I'm surprised that they even bothered to read my proposal.

"No."

"Thomas Fleming, the CEO, happens to be one of the nicest men I've ever met. He's like the grandfather everyone wishes they had. And do you know who his grandson is? Who is slated to take over the family business?"

"Oh no."

"Yep."

"David the douche? Gah, just saying his name makes my skin crawl."

I nod at her statement as I open the lid of the box and start pulling out the supplies inside, placing them on my desk.

"I probably shouldn't go. This has bad news written all over it," I say to Sofie as I look over to her, clasping a pencil between my hands.

I watch as Sofie's signature smirk grows on her pink lips and she fists her hands on her hips.

"No, you know what this has written all over it?"

"What's that?"

"Redemption."

"Huh?"

"Think about it. David allowed his friends to treat you like dirt. Now, this could be your chance to show them that they didn't hold you back or ruin your life. That you're better than you ever were. And you could probably hold their business in the palm of your hand."

"Hmm. . .redemption." I let the word tumble through my mind as a smile grows on my face to match my friend's. "I like it. Alright, I'll do it. When is the meeting?"

"Oh, um. . ." she begins as she pulls out her phone and clicks away. "Today, at two, at their headquarters."

Glancing down at my watch, I look back up at Sofie in a panic and drop the pencil in my hand as I swerve around the desks to go inside the house.

"Sofie, I'll let you organize everything," I shout toward her over my shoulder, hoping that I had the sense to dry clean my suit before I packed it up.

I park my small car in a parking lot across the street from the Fleming headquarters. I glance out my window to the sign posted at the entrance with the fee for the lot and realize that it is going to cost me far more money than necessary.

"You can do this," I whisper to myself as I smooth my hands down my navy suit pants trying to press out a wrinkle that persistently stayed after I ran an iron over it. With a few minutes to spare, I flip down the visor and check my makeup one last time, loving the way the purple silk blouse makes my hazel eyes pop. If I'm going to face the devil, then I'm going to do it looking fabulous.

The alarm on my watch beeps as I reach over to grab my briefcase and make my way across the street to the massive concrete and marble building before me. Once inside, I take a moment to admire the gold and white marble columns against the black marble flooring. The lobby screams mid-century modern and I feel like I'm walking into Oden's temple as a mere mortal disguised as a Goddess. A lamb in wolf's clothing.

An enormous black marble desk flanks the far wall where two receptionists man the station.

"Hello, how can I help you?" the young woman says as I approach.

"Hi, I'm here for a meeting with Fleming Coffee, please. Blake Holliday."

She clicks away at her keyboard and smiles as she pulls up the meeting and hands me a visitor tag with my name prominently displayed.

"You'll take the elevator to the sixth floor. A secretary will greet you when you arrive."

"Thank you," I reply as I make my way to the bank of elevators.

With a deep breath, I press the golden button hoping that I'm not going to regret seizing this opportunity. But without it, I'm not sure how I'll keep the business running or my father's bills paid.

Stepping inside, I give myself a mental pep talk as the car rises.

You can do this. You're the best there is. Put on your big girl panties and show them what you're made of.

Just as I calm myself the doors open and I'm met with a young man whose glasses are sitting just a bit askew on his nose making him look a little harried. Hell, if he works for David, he probably is out of sorts. The lobby on the sixth floor is just as decadent as the one on the main floor.

"Ms. Holliday?" His voice cracks at my last name.

"Yes, that's me."

I watch as he swipes his hands down his pants before nodding and then silently asking me to follow him. I step in line behind him and walk down a long hallway before he knocks on the door once then scurries away as if he is a frightened animal.

The door opens in front of me as my confused gaze follows the retreating back of the man. I have a moment of panic that seizes me, but I remember my mental pep talk in the elevator and continue forward into the room.

"Blake, it's so good to see you." I'm welcomed warmly by the familiar voice of Thomas Fleming. Thomas is reaching his mid-seventies but he doesn't look a day over fifty. And with his black hair peppered with gray, he gives a whole new meaning to the term silver fox.

I almost rush into his arms extended in a hug, but they quickly fall back to his sides as if remembering where he is.

"It's good to see you too, Mr. Fleming."

At the sound of my response, I hear the low conversations in the room fall to silence.

"What's going on?" someone asks, and I have to wonder if it's David.

"I was waiting for one last representative to arrive," Thomas starts as he gestures me into the room. A room filled with testosterone."Everyone, this is Blake. Her company is also here for the contract bid."

My eyes scan the room but immediately fall back to the stormy green gaze of my worst nightmare, Zack, who seems to be equally confused by the interaction. Beside him David sits stewing, the pinched expression on his face diminishing the good looks I remembered from our time together.

I take the offered seat across from my competition and listen as Thomas introduces the rest of the people in the room; most are directors and other executives. Zack and I seem to be the only ones in the office here to bid on the marketing contract.

Just as the room begins to settle after the introductions, David takes a moment to spring out of his chair and slam his fists onto the table.

Looking at his grandfather, he angrily spews accusations. "I thought this was my project. I was going to get to take the lead."

I turn my attention to Thomas, but my skin prickles and the hairs on the back of my neck stand on end, making me wish that I had opted to wear my hair down instead of up in an elegant twist. I've felt this sensation before, but it's been years since it held this kind of power over me. The power to knock me off of my senses.

"It is, and you are. But it's my company, and I still have a say in the matter."

"Well, we had agreed that Zack's company was the best in the business."

"We did, three months ago, before Blake started her own company. And I can tell you, I am very impressed by what I've seen so far."

"So, what is this now? Some sort of grudge match?" David hollers at his grandfather who pins his grandson with a steely gaze.

With a soft knock on the table, I wait for twelve pairs of eyes to journey toward me, giving me their undivided attention.

"Gentlemen, I have a simple solution. Let the best person win."

GOD, SHE'S GORGEOUS WHEN SHE'S RILED up. It reminds me of all the times I used to try to get her attention by doing something just to piss her off. Many of our mentor program sessions in college went that way, much to the chagrin of our mentor. I'd purposefully mess up our campaigns or not complete my portion of the storyboard until the last minute. Whatever I could do just to have her notice me. It was dumb, and it went against every bro code that there is, but something about Blake sparked something inside of me.

She also knew how to give it back, which is what always kept that ember burning. She had no problem calling me out for missed work or for the revolving door of my "harem" as she called it. For the most part, David would try to keep us out of the same room. He always claimed it was so he could have a peaceful evening, but I have a sneaking suspicion he felt a bit jealous of the fiery effect that we had on one another.

Seeing her now though, in her blue suit with the purple shirt that makes her hazel eyes shine even brighter, her hair pulled away from the oval shape of her face highlighting the sleek lines of her neck, everything I thought I had forgotten about this woman comes rushing back. And I hate it.

She's a distraction that I don't need. A distraction that I can't have at this point in my life.

I've worked my ass off for the past six years growing and climbing up the corporate ladder, not to be knocked off course by a headstrong girl wanting to play with the boys.

"Excuse me?" I hear her voice laced in ice linger in the silent room. It spears through me straight to my spine.

"What I mean is, this is the big time, Ms. Holliday, not an assistant's gig where you get to give your two cents on the final project. The scope of this campaign will require your full attention one hundred percent of the time and it has to be new and fresh."

"Are you questioning my capabilities, Mr. Nicholson? Because let me assure you, I've launched numerous campaigns on my own and have the skills and time to devote to it. I also graduated with honors, and at the conclusion of my internship with Sage International Marketing I was offered a Campaign Manager role. Can you say the same?"

God, she is fucking beautiful. And she has me pinned. I didn't graduate with honors, but I did walk out of my internship with a non-entry level job in my hand.

"Everyone," Thomas chimes in, obviously noticing how heated the exchanges are becoming and trying to bring the attention back to the potential campaign. "What we plan to do for this campaign bid is a bit unconventional and will require your time inside and outside of your normal business hours."

"What do you mean, sir?" I ask, concerned with the way this conversation is heading. David may be my best friend, but he's a slimy son-of-a-bitch that loves to work people over and mistreat them.

"David, please give these two a glimpse of what we plan to do to select the company to represent us. . . for the next ten years."

"A ten-year contract?" Blake whispers to herself, her eyes growing wide with surprise and as they focus more, I can see a hint of hope.

What kind of story do you have to tell, beautiful girl? I think to myself.

"Yes, as I said – unconventional. David, please." He gestures to his grandson as he takes a seat at the head of the table and David stands.

I can see the gears spinning in David's head. He was thrown a wrench when Blake walked in moments ago, thinking that the campaign would automatically go to me, but he's already concocting a new plan. I'm not sure what happened between the two of them, I just know that he despises her as much as she despises him.

I remember watching her storm out of the fraternity house after catching David sleeping with another blonde bimbo, many of whom I had wanted to tell her about, but my best friend had sworn me to secrecy, claiming that it would only hurt Blake to know what he was doing behind her back. I was stupid and listened. But I couldn't quite ever figure out why he hated her so much so many years later. I always just thought he was mad that he got caught and she was the one that dumped him, instead of the other way around. I missed the big breakup, my science lab was scheduled during the time, but the brothers gave him shit for two days – what about precisely, I'm not sure. At that point I was too busy preparing myself to move on in the world. Then the Vice President found out he knocked up two girls around the same time and David became old news, which seemed to piss him off even more.

But as I watch his eyes narrow and a devious grin grow on his lips, I know that there has to have been something more that went on while I was getting dressed that fateful morning, but I never asked any questions. All of my memories lie in the hurtful stare of the girl that saw me carrying a random phone I had found in the bathroom that morning out of my bedroom and watching the weight of the world fall onto her shoulders.

A weight that seems to have grown tenfold in the last six years. It makes me wonder what secrets she's harboring.

"You called this a grudge match, and perhaps that is the best term to use. Two rival companies competing against each other to secure a ten-year contract for one of the fastest growing cafes and companies in the country. So, now ask yourself. What are you willing to do to secure this contract?"

My eyes narrow into slants as I gaze at David. The snake so many claim him to be was coming out from behind his bush.

"First, we want you all to get an idea of what it's like in every division of this company. Get a real insider's view of what it takes to run it from the ground up."

I can get on board with that. It's not the first time a company has suggested that when launching a new campaign.

Continuing, David says, "First, you'll both be spending a day as an intern, for me. Then we'll have you work two days at one of our slowest cafes before moving you to one of our busiest. Finally, you will have the opportunity to shadow my grandfather for a day to learn what it has taken to build the company from the ground up and make it the success that it is. Any questions so far?"

I peek at Blake out of the corner of my eye and I can see that she is working hard to hold back a saucy grin. David must have forgotten that she worked at a coffee shop in college. The drinks were terrible, but the drinks weren't the reason I would go. It was to see her and maybe to see if I could rile her up for the day.

"Good. Along with the campaigns, we plan to use the marketing firm chosen as our event planners. As you probably know, every year we host a large scale New Year's Eve party for our employees, investors, and patrons who wish to buy tickets. Those funds are donated to a selected charity every year. Together, you will plan this event."

"That's in two months," Blake points out, mirroring my concern.

"You are correct. We want to see what you can do under pressure. And I assure you, if the party is not up to our standards, then we will make the decision to move forward without either of you."

I let the tasks sit and settle in my mind for a moment. When they said this would be unconventional, they weren't joking. Most of the time I head into a meeting ready to wow the group with a few sample campaigns and walk out not long after with a signed deal in hand. I should have known David wouldn't make this easy. Or, I suppose I should blame Thomas for pulling the rug out from under myself, David, and Blake. None of us were expecting the other.

"And what about our other projects?" I ask.

"You'll have a lot of late nights to prove to us how well you can multitask. Our goal is to grow internationally. If you can't handle a campaign like this at a national expansion, how can you manage it at a global level?"

He makes a good point, unfortunately. I'll have to discuss it with my director to see how he feels about handing off some of my smaller projects so that I can focus on the larger ones. David's plan really throws me off my game. He doesn't realize that before this meeting today I was told that if we land this gig, I would be looking at a major promotion. Now my best friend is standing in the way of that, right behind the girl that caught my eye ten years ago when she walked into our freshman introduction to marketing class. Because if anyone is going to knock me off my game, it's her.

"Are there any other questions?" Thomas asks as he joins his grandson at the head of the table.

"When will this begin?" I question.

"Oh yes, I would like to see you both here tomorrow at nine sharp."

Blake and I both nod our heads as we stand and gather our belongings.

"One more thing," Thomas adds as a few of the executives shake our hands. "I would appreciate it if this remains civil. Yes, you're competing against each other, but this is a family company, and I would like to keep the bloodshed down to a minimum."

"Yes, sir," Blake and I chime in at the same time.

David and Thomas wait for the rest of the executives to file out of the room before escorting us in the same manner.

"I apologize that I don't have the chance to catch up with either of you this afternoon. I'm heading to another meeting. I look forward to seeing what you both come up with."

Thomas shakes my hand and then Blake's, but I don't miss the way he gently pats Blake on the shoulder as he turns around to leave. It's a touch of paternal affection, and it leaves Blake smiling at his retreat. But that smile quickly diminishes as she turns her attention back to David and myself.

"I'll see you gentlemen tomorrow," she utters as she spins on her stilettos and makes her way to the front of the offices.

"Hey, Blake, wait up. I'll ride down with you," I call out, earning me an eye roll, and I can vaguely hear her mutter, "Great."

"What are you doing, man? Don't mess this up. I'm going to make sure that you win this contract but I need you to keep your distance from the competition. Man, I still can't believe my grandfather pulled that shit today."

"I'm not worried, David. I'll blow them away."

That damn sinister look gleams again in his eye and I'm thankful that I'm not on the receiving end.

"Oh, don't worry. I'm going to make sure of it."

As I turn my retreating back to him and head toward the elevators, I call out, "Don't do anything stupid."

I probably need to tell myself the same. Because if there was anyone that would make me do something stupid, it would be the woman standing at the bank of elevators tapping the toe of her heeled shoe on the marble floor while she stares at me silently telling me to "Fuck off."

"Hello, beautiful," I tell her as I step up beside her just as the elevator doors open.

"Don't call me that," she spews as she reaches her delicate hand out to press the button for the ground floor. The pale pink polish of her nails is in complete contradiction to the rest of her. She's covered herself in a suit of armor to show that she's hard, strong, and determined while the pastel color on her fingertips scream that she's soft, pliable, and sensitive. The question is, which side of her turns me on the most?

I step into her space and continue to follow her retreating figure as she presses herself against the wall of the elevator.

"What would you prefer that I call you? Angel, sweetheart, cupcake? Pick your choice."

"You could use my first name? I have it for a reason."

"No, I think I'll keep calling you beautiful."

She rolls her eyes and crosses her arms against her chest as she murmurs, "Whatever."

On a whim, I reach out and press the stop button on the elevator and the car jerks as it halts. Blake's eyes turn to me in panic and anger.

"What are you doing?" she cries out as she tries to reach around me to press the button for the ground floor again.

"Why do you hate me so much, Blake?" I question as I pin her arms above her head and lean into her space. Her chest rises and falls with each breath, those succulent mounds trying to burst free from her blouse. I force myself to keep my attention on her face, her eyes have always been the key to figuring out how she really feels. And right now they're filled with confusion, anger, and fear.

"What?"

"For four years you looked at me as if I was the scum of the earth and I want to know why."

"Because you were an asshole to me pretty much every day for four years."

"You were the asshole first, beautiful," I remind her as I reach down and sweep aside a piece of wispy hair that has fallen loose from the knot she has twisted it in.

Her silence speaks more than she'll ever know, the volume almost deafening.

Just as I'm about to question her again the elevator car jerks and she reaches up to grip my forearms in panic. Her eyes widen to the size of saucers as the car shakes then begins its descent once more. She stares up at me and I find myself hypnotized by her gaze. Without deliberation, I lean forward wanting to taste her more than my last breath. But with luck not on my side, the doors of the elevator open and Blake scoots out from under my stance and scurries off through the lobby as if someone has set the place on fire.

The only thing on fire right now is the fucking ember of attraction I have toward Blake that I was sure had been extinguished years ago. The moment she walked into that conference room this morning and I heard her voice, smelled her sweet perfume she's worn since college, I was a goner.

And fuck me, I hate it.

W WITH HUNCHED SHOULDERS, I WALK into the converted garage of my father's house. I didn't expect for David to twist the contract opportunity the way that he did. I mean, I'm not surprised, but I simply didn't expect it. If Thomas, or any of the other executives, hadn't been in the room I would have given the slimeball a piece of my mind. Instead, I was forced to sit quietly and listen to his full-blown scheme in an attempt to embarrass me. Didn't he know that I planned to rule the world? Apparently, he didn't get the memo because I plan to show these boys what I'm capable of.

"Hey, how'd it go? Did you lock them in?" Sofie asks as I toss my scarf onto the coat rack and then follow it with my wool coat, both of which I wished I had taken into the meeting with me earlier. When I scurried out of the building, a chill had filled the air. It's not even Thanksgiving and the temperatures have been dropping steadily to the point where the meteorologists are calling for snow before Christmas. And I hate snow. That was part of the reason I jumped at the chance to intern in Georgia. It wasn't to escape my college scandal as everyone had suspected.

"It was good. Interesting."

"How so?"

I take a deep breath and try to figure out how to say this without sending Sofie off the deep end. She's always been my biggest supporter, and I'm afraid she may do something drastic. Castration is a threat often verbalized by my friend.

"Well, it seems Zack was there as well."

"Okay, that I suspected," she says with a hint of relief.

"Oh, that's not the worst part." I delve into the meeting and describe how David whined like a petulant child until his grandfather gave him the opportunity to manipulate the bidding process however he wanted.

When I finish telling her about my morning, she stares at me completely dumbfounded.

As the initial shock wears off, Sofie runs a hand through her sleek blonde hair and asks, "What are you going to do?"

"I'm going to do what I do best. Work my ass off, pray that the nurse shows up every day to take care of dad, and plan one hell of a New Year's Eve party."

"What about the work you're already doing? I don't want you to run yourself ragged."

Her concern is overwhelming and heartfelt. I find myself walking toward her and wrapping my arms around her waist.

"I'll be fine. It's nothing that I can't handle. And Sofie, I haven't told you the best news." She cocks her eyebrow at me skeptically, silently asking me to continue. "If I win this bid, then we're locked into a ten-year contract to expand their brand internationally."

"Seriously?" she gasps as her hand travels to cover her mouth in surprise.

"Yep," I reply, popping the "p" with my lips.

"Well, fuck me sideways."

Bouncing on my toes, I let the idea of winning the contract actually seep in, and the elation begins to blossom. "I can't believe it."

Sofie grips my shoulders tightly and joins in my bouncing, and before we know it, we've turned on her phone to play a few classic boy band songs as we're dancing in our office.

"I hope that I'm not disturbing you," a deep voice bellows from the entrance to the house and we both spin around grinning widely.

"Hi, Daddy. How did therapy go today?" Sliding over to my father, I kiss him on the cheek and he answers with a grin.

"That woman is determined to make me cry out in pain. I want a new nurse."

My dad has been complaining about his nurse since she started a few weeks back. I think he's secretly harboring a crush on her.

"She's the best in town, so you're going to have to deal with Maggie whether you like it or not. You're lucky that she puts up with you."

My father grumbles at my statement as he wheels himself farther into the garage turning himself around to take in the finished space. Though my father had someone set the room up to be livable, I worked by myself to paint, lay flooring, and add the shelving and desks to make it a space that I'm proud of. I told my father he couldn't see it until I was done. Now it screams classic, clean, and modern.

The space is mostly white, with dark flooring covered by a cream-colored and navy rug, two glass desks with white chairs and gray cushions. Hints of gold and brass are scattered throughout. My favorite feature though is probably the seating area I set up. It has a small cream-colored loveseat with a glass coffee table adorned with pink peonies and a gold catch-all bowl. Behind it is a window looking out to the mountain view behind my father's house anchored by two floor to ceiling bookshelves embellished with books, candles, and knickknacks.

"This looks great. You did a good job, sweetie."

"Thanks, Dad. And thank you for letting us work out of here. It saves us a lot of money by not having to rent office space."

"You know that I'm happy to have you close. Now, what's for dinner?"

"Dad, I just got home from a really important meeting."

"Oh yeah?"

I gaze over to Sofie who is sitting at her desk working on her laptop and she gives me a thumbs up.

"Well, I may be. . .I mean, hopefully. . .BH Marketing is bidding on a ten-year contract with Fleming Coffee to take them coastal, national, and hopefully international," I finally let out in one breath.

I wait patiently for my father's reaction as I rock in place with my hands clasped in front of my chest.

"Wow," he whispers. "That's the best news I've heard in weeks, sweetie. You shouldn't be here about to make us dinner. You should be out celebrating."

"Oh, Dad. It's not locked in yet. I won't know for another two months. In the meantime, my ex is running us in circles."

"Your ex?"

"Oh yes, that's the caveat. He's the Vice President or something and his grandfather is letting him choose between his best friend, who is my competition, or me. The Board of Directors has a say, but ultimately it is David's and Mr. Fleming's choice."

Just saying it out loud has the anger rushing back into my veins. I'm hoping that whatever hate David has toward me, which is completely unjustified, stays out of the race. But I'm not stupid enough to know that he won't pick Zack. My hope is that everyone else outweighs his vote.

The room goes silent as my father ruminates on what I've just told him.

"Well, I still think you should celebrate. This is a huge opportunity for you."

"What will you do?"

"Don't worry about me. I have about fifty casseroles in the fridge ready to be eaten."

"Only if you're sure."

"Positive. Now you and Sofie go have a few drinks. I'll be fine."

I watch as my father wheels himself back out of the space, his demeanor surprising me. When I was younger, he kept me on a tight leash. No going out, no friendly get-togethers, and I was to come home right after school and that was where I was to stay. He was even that way when I would come home on college breaks. If I stayed in his house, I had to obey his rules. I guess the accident threw him for a loop and he realized how short life is.

Breaking from my trance, I shake my head as Sofie calls me over to her desk.

"So, I worked some things around your calendar and I think we can manage to fit in the eight hour days at Fleming Coffee that you mentioned and give you time to work on the six other campaigns we have floating around. I can manage office duties here, and if we need to schedule calls or meetings, we'll work through it then."

"Wow, Sofie, this is great. Thank you. I think this is totally doable. And if David wants to be a dick about it then I'll just go to Mr. Fleming. This may actually help prove to them that I can balance it all."

"Now that we have that part covered, let's go to FIA and have some fun."

FIA is our favorite bar in the small downtown of Hollisville and is owned by our friend Samantha. It literally stands for Fuck It All which makes us love it even more.

"Ok, let me change and we can head out."

Two hours later Sofie and I sit at a high top table with a spread of chicken wings, cheesy fries, and tall glasses of beer between us. We've both had two and are feeling good enough that I'm actually considering calling a pick up for tonight.

"Sofie, did I tell you how good he looked?"

With a fry hanging from her mouth she looks up at me with a pinched confused expression. "David?" she says around a mouth full of cheesy potato.

"No, you dummy. Zack. God, Sofie, I swear he looks better now than he did in college."

"Oh . . . Zack. He was always too damn hot for the likes of the women he kept around. Are you admitting your crush on him finally?"

"I didn't have a crush on Zack."

Oh, I'm lying, I totally did have the hots for the boy and I hope that she can't tell behind my reddening cheeks.

"Girl, everyone had a crush on Zack. How could you not? I'm pretty sure most of the guys had a crush on him too."

"If you had a thing for him then why didn't you go after him?"

"Oh, Blake," she says as if she's speaking to a child. "That boy only had eyes for you."

With the glass of beer resting against my lips, I fight the urge to spit the drink back out. I forcefully swallow the cold liquid.

"What? He did not. I was dating his best friend, and he hated me, remember?"

"That boy loved you. Everyone knew it."

"You're crazy. I think I need to cut you off. You've had too much to drink."

Before I have a chance to think any harder about Zack maybe, potentially, being attracted to me in college, Sofie's eyes light up and she perks up in her seat.

"Hmm. . . I bet he still does," she whispers as she waves at a newcomer.

"Who are you waving at?" I ask her as I turn on my stool to lock eyes with the last person I want to see today. I avert my gaze quickly and spin back around in my seat. And, of course, the irrational part of me looks down at my ripped boyfriend jeans and off-the-shoulder sweater wondering why I had to go for comfort when Sofie and I decided to celebrate tonight while she looks like a million bucks across the table. And why the hell am I feeling jealous of Sofie?

"Hello, ladies," Zack says as he approaches.

Sofie jumps down from her chair and embraces my enemy before repeating his greeting.

"Long time no see, Sofie. Are you back for good?"

"Just moved back from New York to work with Blake."

Cutting into their riveting conversation, I bluntly ask, "What are you doing here, Zack? You don't live in this town."

He pins his gaze onto me but I don't falter, I remain stoic in my question.

"Can't a guy come to check out a new bar?"

"No. Now leave."

"Oh, Blake, you don't mean that. We probably need to spend some time catching up since we'll be working so closely together for the next two months."

"You mean me working and you screwing around while David tries to sabotage everything?"

"Not true. I won't screw anything unless you ask me to." He winks, and from across the table, I hear Sofie sigh. Turning my head, I see her with her elbow resting on the table and her chin placed delicately in her hand, her gaze fascinated by our exchange.

"Why are you really here, Zack? As much as I'm enjoying our enthralling conversation, I was having a great evening until about five minutes ago."

"I'm here to see Samantha."

My chest pinches and twists at the mention of my friend's name. Samantha is beautiful with her short stance and pink pixie haircut. She and Zack would look perfect together. His dark to her light. But a tiny smidgen of jealousy flares and I can't control the filter on my words before they're cascading from my mouth.

"Oh, is she your latest conquest? Do I need to fill her in on all of your escapades while you were in college, a ritual I'm certain that you continue today? I mean, I figured it would be something you would grow out of –,"
I spew until he yanks me by my arm and tugs me off my

stool and across the bar. The hallway leading to the bathroom comes into view and I look over my shoulder in panic toward Sofie but she sits with a happy dazed expression on her face as she waves in my direction.

"What are you doing?" I bark at him, but Zack doesn't respond. Instead, he pulls me toward the dark end of the hallway and then forcefully spins me around so that my back is against the paneling-covered wall, my chest brushing against his. Zack's gaze is heated, whether from anger or passion, I'm unsure, but it's hypnotizing.

"I'm doing this," he growls as his hand reaches up to grasp my chin in his palm. Tilting my head back, he captures my lips with his own. I'm stunned at first, but the sparks igniting beneath his touch have me mimicking every brush of his lips. And when his tongue peeks out for a taste, I answer the call by allowing the intrusion. Zack swipes his tongue against mine and a groan echoes in the hallway, one I recognize as my own. Suddenly my skin feels hot, burning, torturous as he slides his hand from my chin down toward the back of my neck, tingles following his every movement.

His kiss has taken me by surprise and just when I start to reach out to test and see if his body is as taut as I remember, he pulls away from me completely. He looks at me with a coldness in his eyes that I never would have expected and it feels like someone has poured ice water all over my skin.

"Samantha is my cousin, Blake. I appreciate you thinking so highly of me," he menacingly barks. "I'll see you tomorrow."

As he turns his back to me, my blood boils. "What was this, Zack? I didn't want you to kiss me."

"Yes, you did."

Damn him, I so did, which confuses me even more. I'm not one to be spontaneous, I've always had too much to lose. I take my time and come up with decisions after a lot of consideration of the consequences. That's probably why I haven't dated since David. Because the last time I thought irrationally I ended up regretting something that I can't ever take back.

I watch as Zack reaches across the bar to hug Samantha and even though I know that they're related now, I can't help but feel jealous. Not because of the affection he is showing her, but because of the way his body relaxes entirely and his eyes light up. Something I've never been on the receiving end of.

As I walk toward them after exiting the hallway, making sure that my sweater isn't askew, Zack turns toward me and winks.

"I hate you," I murmur to him as I stomp past them.

"I know, beautiful."

I swear that I hear someone else growling in my ear, it's not me. It can't be. But as I sit back down on my stool, Sofie looks at me and laughs.

"You look like you're ready to claw someone's eyes out."

"Shut up. How did we not know that Samantha is Zack's cousin?"

She turns to look at them, Samantha speaking animatedly to Zack as he throws his head back in laughter. I almost wish that he hadn't worn his suit because no man can wear a suit like Zack. It molds to his body like a second skin.

"I can see the resemblance. And we don't really know Samantha all that well. When we get together none of us discuss family."

Resigned, I take a sip of my beer. "You're right."

"So, what did you two do in the hallway?" Sofie inquires as she leans across the table.

"Nothing. It was just stupid. So stupid."

"What was?"

"He kissed me."

Her eyes and smile grow double in size.

"Did you kiss him back?"

I don't respond. Instead, I lay my head on the table and gently bang it a few times repeating to myself that I'm an idiot.

"How could I do something so foolish?"

"Because. . .you still have a thing for him?"

"I hate him, Sofie. I hate him so much."

I KNEW ONCE SAMANTHA SAW ME EXIT THE hallway quickly, followed by the evil glare of Blake, my cousin would have questions. Particularly ones that I have zero desire to answer.

"So, how do you know Blake?" Samantha asks just as I turn back around from calling Blake her new nickname.

"She's just someone I'm working on a project with."

"Mmhmm. I don't believe that for one second."

"It's true. David is her ex and we're both bidding on a contract for his grandfather's company."

"Oh, now the pieces are falling into place," she says dramatically.

"Just drop it, Sam. You're looking for something that isn't there. She hates me and I equally despise her."

Even though the years have passed, my reasonings for hating Blake seemed foggier. But the feeling was there, permeating through my memories of our years in college.

"Doth protest too much."

"Shush. Now, since you dragged me all the way out here, I'll take a beer and hear whatever idea you've concocted for the family Christmas party."

Samantha begins diving into an elaborate plan to bring all of our family together as part of a reunion, but to surprise my parents with it. Besides Samantha, everyone else in our family lives on the west coast. My father took a job in Charlottesville when I was a baby and we've called it home ever since. Samantha came to visit us four years ago and never left.

Her arms start flailing about as she goes into all of the minute details she's created in her mind and I can't help but throw my head back and laugh.

"What's so funny? This is serious business."

"Look, Samantha. I'm on board with whatever you decide to do, just give me my to-do list, and I'll check it off."

"Well, I thought that would take a bit more convincing on my part."

"Why? My parents would love to see their siblings, and it's their thirtieth anniversary too. I can't think of a better gift to give them. I'm going to be slammed for the next two months but whatever you need, just ask."

"Well, if you insist. I need you to be in charge of the food. Can you find a caterer?"

"Yeah, I'm on it." Samantha claps her hands together in excitement and then walks over to the beer tap and dispenses a glass of my favorite brew before placing it in front of me.

"She's leaving."

Without question, I turn around and watch as Blake and Sofie gather their jackets and leave a few dollars on the table top as a tip. Before they walk out the door, Blake must feel my eyes on her. She looks over her shoulder and scowls in my direction before stomping through the exit.

"Oh, this is going to be fun."

Ignoring my cousin, I ask, "She's not driving, is she?"

"Worried?" At my blank expression, Samantha continues, "No, Blake doesn't drink more than one and drive. They called a car about thirty minutes ago. You're lucky that we're friends."

"Stop reading into it, Samantha. I'd have the same concern if it were Sofie."

"Whatever you say. I've got work to do. This one's on the house, I'll see you later."

"Thanks."

I sip the beer then set the cool glass between my hands, watching the frothy head of the brew dissolve into the liquid beneath. This feeling of disdain that I have toward Blake surprises me, especially as it battles against my attraction for her. It's as if my emotions are waging war and my heart may be the one with the ultimate downfall.

What is it about her that has me wishing that things were different? Wishing that I didn't equally hate being in her presence but yearning for it all the same. Is it her striking beauty that any man gifted with sight can attest to or is it her fiery personality and spirit hiding beneath her shy exterior? Whatever it is, it's fighting a battle within me that I have no intention of losing.

Blake made it a point to treat me no better than scum since the day we met, and for that reason, I need to do whatever I can to make sure she doesn't stand a chance at stealing this contract away from me. This opportunity means more than just a hefty promotion and raise for me, it means finally proving something to my family and taking care of them the way they've always taken care of me.

I wonder what's in it for Blake. Besides the opportunity to snag a contract for ten years, she was bound and determined to prove herself in the meeting today. She's always been quiet yet resolute and firm, one of the things that attracted me to her the most when we were in class together. But today there seemed to be something more behind her tenacity, something pushing her steadily toward this goal come hell or high water.

"Excuse me," a sultry voice says from beside me, and I turn to find a very attractive woman standing beside my stool. Her plump lips are painted in the same shade of red as her formfitting dress. "Would you care to buy me a drink?" she suggests as she leans into my space.

The scent of her floral perfume wafts into my space, and though the scent is pleasant, it's all wrong. The only woman's scent I want to inhale is the one belonging to a female hell-bent on putting me in my place.

"Sure," I tell the stranger as I slide off the stool and offer her my seat in the now crowded bar. "Sam? This lady's drink is on me," I shout above the crowd and watch as my cousin looks at me in confusion and then nods her head.

"Thank you," the woman purrs as she drags a dark fingernail across the sleeve of my suit jacket.

"You're welcome. Enjoy your night," I tell her as I turn away from the bar, leaving the woman with a surprised expression on her overly made-up face. It's probably the first time she's ever been turned down. I hate to be the one to do it, but there is only one woman's attention I crave and right now, she's most likely sitting at home plotting a hundred different ways to kill me with a pencil.

Outside I stand in the crisp, breezy air letting the chill soak through my clothing and sting against my skin. The night is still young, and I know I should head home to get some rest before David decides to proceed with his pissing match, but I find myself wondering if Blake and Sofie made it home okay. It would be gentlemanly of me to check on them.

Snagging my phone from my pocket, I immediately dial my assistant's number. It's past her working hours but she was briefed today with the extent of this project and she offered to assist me when needed. This may be outside the realm of business, but I'm willing to risk it.

"Hello, Mr. Nicholson. What can I do for you?"

"I need you to get me someone's cell phone number."

"Really?" she inquires and I can hear her grin blossoming. Cathy is around the same age as my parents and has been pleading with me to find a nice girl to settle down with.

"Yes."

"Zack," she says warmly but with a questioning tone, "is this for business or pleasure?"

Chuckling I reply, "Both. Blake Holliday is the owner of my competition for the Fleming contract. We also went to college together. I saw her tonight at my cousin Samantha's bar and she and her friend took a ride home. I just want to make sure she got home safely."

"Your mother raised a good boy. And though I have a suspicion of there being an ulterior motive, I'm going to let it slide. I'll message you the number in a minute."

"Thank you, Cathy."

"You're welcome. And good luck tomorrow. You're going to need it." She ends the call with a laugh.

As I'm walking to my car, I hear a ping on my phone, and I look down to see a phone number as well as a link to Blake's social media page. Why I never looked her up before now, I'm not sure. Probably because I had hoped to move on from my college infatuation with her. Or maybe I was afraid to see her happy with someone else. Either way, until this moment I had never come across her page and my thumb hesitates at pressing the link to pull it up on my phone's browser.

Taking a deep breath, I press the link and a picture of her smiling face beside Sofie's in front of the Empire State Building fills the screen. This is the Blake I crave, the one that's happy and carefree. The one that lets her hair down and enjoys life. I've seen it a couple of times before but that smile was never for me, she keeps it stowed away for her close friends and family.

Closing the browser, I tap on the phone number, save it in my contacts, and then prompt my phone to send a message.

Zack: Hey. I just wanted to check on you.

I send the message and then pile into my car, turning on the ignition to warm up a bit.

Beautiful Girl: Who is this?

Zack: Your favorite person.

Beautiful Girl: Well, my favorite person is currently indisposed. So, let's try again.

Zack: Ok, your least favorite person?

Beautiful Girl: That narrows it down to two of you and since I had the displeasure of running into one of you tonight, I am going to assume this is Zack.

Zack: Ding Ding, we have a winner.

Beautiful Girl: Please don't message me again.

Zack: Hey, I just wanted to make sure that you and Sofie made it home safely. That's it.

I watch the small bubbles pop up and then disappear on my screen and I know that I've stumped her with my thoughtfulness. After a minute of not receiving a response, I place my phone onto the passenger seat and put the car in drive heading back home.

The journey isn't long, about thirty minutes or so, but about five minutes after I get on the road I hear my phone ping and I am praying that it's Blake responding. With my luck it will be David, being the douche that he is, demanding me to join him and whomever he is without to some bar downtown.

Pulling into my gravel driveway, I take a moment to admire the small ranch farmhouse I purchased about a year ago. I hired a team to renovate the century-old property and just this past month the renovations have been completed. Which was great because living with my parents for a year really took a toll on my bachelorhood. Not that there had been many women before that. Despite what Blake and David have always believed, I'm not as big a playboy as I appear. Most of the women in college typically came to me and then passed out. After college, I was always too busy working my way up the corporate ladder to date or do more than have a casual hookup.

Clicking the button for the garage door, I anxiously pull my car into the spot, nearly colliding with the wall on the opposite side in my haste to read my missed message.

"Come on, man. It's just a girl," I whisper in the car as I press the stop button on the dash, killing the ignition.

In the darkness of the garage, I take a deep breath and then another until I feel a sense of calm wash over me. Reaching blindly across the center console I dig around on the seat until my hand touches the cool plastic and glass of my phone. I instinctually press the power button and the screen's light fills the car in a blue glow.

The air escapes from my lungs as I see my missed message is from Blake.

Beautiful Girl: Wow, you actually took me by surprise. I'm not sure how to feel about that. On the one hand I'd like to think that under the assholishness that you actually have feelings, but then on the other, I think that you're using the knowledge that I'm home to come kill me in my sleep.

Beautiful Girl: You can see my dilemma.

> Beautiful Girl: Uh oh, ten minutes with no response. Guess that means I should sleep with a light on.

I can't help but laugh at her banter, something she and I have never exchanged in person.

> Zack: Sorry, beautiful. I had a 30-minute drive home. Glad to hear that you're safe. . .from me. . .for now. <insert evil laugh>

> Zack: I'm just kidding. I wouldn't do well in prison. Orange isn't my color.

> Zack: And I wouldn't have anyone's day to ruin.

> Beautiful Girl: So true. I'm going to bed. I'm sure David has a splendid day planned for tomorrow.

Unable to help myself I chuckle as I reply with a new message.

> Zack: What are you wearing?

> Beautiful Girl: Fuck off.

Inside my house, I throw my bag and keys onto the kitchen counter and make my way to my bedroom where I strip myself naked and climb into bed. I turn my head to look at the empty space beside me and wonder if there is some miraculous way for Blake and me to put our hatred aside for a night or two and ride this attraction out of our system. Because even just a stupid text conversation has my dick harder than it has ever been in my life.

As I close my eyes I consider all of the ways to convince her to come to my bed, but then I think about the way she returned my kiss tonight and I realize that there may not have to be much convincing at all. She wants me as much as I want her.

Because we all know that there is a fine line between hate and love, but lust? That's a whole other ballgame.

RENEE HARLESS

CHAPTER Three

IS BODY CASTS A SHADOW OVER ME even in the darkened hallway. He's close, closer than I should allow, but I can't help myself. I feel a pull toward him, something strong and unexplainable. The kiss is surprising, but not unwelcome. I've craved the chance to learn his taste for years and it doesn't disappoint. A mix of spearmint and something uniquely him.

I'm pressed stock still against the wall, his strong hips holding me in place, the outline of his growing erection pressing against my hip. And it feels glorious. I lose myself in his feeling as his tongue strokes against mine, savoring me the same way that I'm relishing him.

I reach my hands out to feel if he is as taut as he looks but I'm startled awake by a buzzing sound on my nightstand.

"Dammit," I curse in my empty childhood bedroom.

This is the third night this week that I've re-lived that moment with Zack in my dreams. He's been haunting me every night and I wake up feeling more tired than when I put myself to bed the evening before.

Today is the first day Zack and I will actually work as interns. We spent the first day in orientation and making rounds through the office and then the second day Thomas sat with us and went over some of the core features he would like for our initial campaign proposals as well as showing us previous years New Year's galas.

Never being one to mind waking up early, I try my best to stretch in bed and get myself going, but today is a struggle. I'm not sure if it's the lack of sleep or that my body has been buzzing since my encounter with Zack on Monday evening and the subsequent dreams that followed, but either way, I have to force myself out of bed.

Knowing I need to check in on my dad and get a quick workout in, I exchange my pajamas for some gym shorts and a tank top before stepping out of my room and taking the stairs to the basement where I set up a small gym.

I only put in a thirty-minute workout, time isn't on my side, but I feel significantly better now that I've got my blood flowing.

"Dad?" I call out when I reach the top of the stairs and hear a few squeaks coming down the hallway.

"Good morning, sweetie. You're up bright and early."

It's only half past five, and the sun has yet to break through the horizon leaving the sky in a deep shade of blue.

"Yeah, I get to intern for David today. Hooray," I say sullenly, my mock sarcasm gaining a chuckle from my father.

"You'll do fine. You have another person with you too, right?" my dad asks as he wheels himself into the kitchen and begins to grab a few items from the fridge for his breakfast.

"Yes, his best friend, remember? I get the sneaking suspicion that today they're going to gang up on me. I'll probably have to do cartwheels while retrieving coffee for them both."

"Well, you were always great at cartwheels."

"Thanks, Dad. So, what does Maggie have in store for you today?"

"That witch probably has something evil planned."

"Come on, Dad. You're already doing so much better than the doctors anticipated. I'm so grateful for Maggie, don't give her a reason to leave," I scold him as I take a look at the calendar on the side of the refrigerator.

"You have a checkup appointment today. So, behave. No shenanigans when Maggie is driving."

"Yes, Mom," my dad jokes and I playfully swat his shoulder.

"Here, let me make you some eggs. I have some time," I tell him, snagging the egg carton from his grasp. I'm not certain how my father intended to cook since he can't see over the counter in his chair. Unless the meal goes in the oven or the microwave we placed at his level, otherwise it's hopeless.

"That'd be great. Thanks."

After getting my dad settled, I rush into the bathroom to take a quick shower. I don't have the time to luxuriate in the warmth of the spray as I rush through washing my thick chestnut brown hair. I take a few extra minutes to dry and style it into soft waves and run through my five-minute makeup routine.

Back in my room I sift through my closet and settle on a plum-colored long sleeve dress that lands just above my knees. I'm sure that I should probably wear flats today knowing that David is going to have me gallivanting all over the city for God knows what reason, but I opt for a pair of bronze colored heels and drape a necklace of the same color across my chest.

Grabbing my coat, scarf, and purse I call out a goodbye to my father and head out into the brisk fall weather. The moment the chilled air touches my legs a gasp bursts from my lips. I should have thrown on a pair of tights or hose to provide some sort of protection to my bare legs, but I hate wearing those things. I feel like I'm always tugging at them or they're cinching my waist in the worst possible way.

I step into my car and turn over the engine, letting the interior heat up as my teeth chatter and fill the space with the staccato noise. The forecast had been calling for an early snowstorm this weekend, some system traveling down from Canada making its way known, but I think it may pop in a bit sooner. I hope I'm able to get through the day before any of the white stuff starts falling. People tend to panic in our area at the first mention of snow and I'm sure today will be no different.

My toes finally regain feeling, and with the heater kicking into gear, I back my car out of the driveway and make my way to Fleming headquarters.

I arrive a few minutes early and make sure to greet the young man working the desk with a warm smile. I learned on my first official day that his name was Joey and he had been interning for three weeks.

"Good morning, Joey," I call out as I pass the main desk, his glasses permanently askew on his face.

"Hi, Ms. Holliday," his voice screeches. "You can head back to Mr. Fleming, er. . .David's office."

"Thank you."

Walking down the narrow hallway, I stop at the door with David's name engraved on a silver plaque. I raise my hand with the intention of knocking, but I hold back as my fist rests an inch from the wooden door. I'm not sure I'm comfortable being in a room alone with him. Whether it's due to anger or insecurities, or the simple fact that he's trying to make things difficult for me, maybe it's all of those reasons. But I take a step back allowing my fist to fall back down to my side.

"Did the door say something interesting?" I hear the familiar deep voice say behind me. I can almost see the gravely tone skate across my skin leaving a path of goosebumps in its wake. Closing my eyes, I inhale his scent just for a moment; a split-second to let him in and succumb to my body's yearning.

But only for that second or else I risk losing myself to it.

Straightening my spine, I turn to face Zack who stands ever so close with a donut in one hand and a bag in the other. My gaze moves from his face to the powdery food then back to his eyes again.

"What are you doing?"

"Eating and hoping that you'll open the door since my hands are full."

"I'm not your servant."

"Yes, but I'm hoping that nestled beneath all of that anger-fueled hatred is a kind person that would get the door for someone who has their hands full."

A growl sounds from my chest as I hold back the desire to snag the donut from his grasp and smash it in his too good-looking face.

Luckily I'm saved from having to clean up a mess of smashed sugary confections as David's door opens wide with his eyes taking in the closeness of Zack and my proximity. Zack pays him no mind and pushes past the opening and places the paper bag on the corner of David's desk before taking a seat on the small couch along the wall.

"Come in, Blake. I won't bite. . .unless you want me to." David grins and winks at me as I pass.

"Please don't make me file a sexual harassment suit. I really have better things to do with my time."

As he closes the door, I hear him mumble to himself, "God, when did you become such a bitch?"

Knowing he's not expecting a response, I reply, "About the same moment I learned how much of an asshole you are."

"What about me?" Zack asks as I remove my coat and scarf and take the seat across from him.

"What about you?" I snap in return.

"You've always been callous toward me."

Seriously? Does he not remember all the times he would arrive late for our projects or forget them all together? He would call me out for ridiculous things like the clothes that I wore from the local consignment shop because it was more cost effective than buying brand new items. And the fact that I spent all of my free time studying gave him a ticket to ridicule me for not having fun.

"You get what you give."

"Are you two done?" David asks, wanting the attention back on him just like old times, but I can feel Zack's gaze centered on me. "Today I have a few projects typical of our interns. I will be in and out of meetings with some of our investors today, but if you have any questions, you can buzz my secretary. I'll be checking in periodically, so I suggest that you two stay on task because if you fall behind or don't complete today's projects, it will be noted in the contract proposal."

On the one hand I'm thankful that I won't have to answer to David all day, on the other I'll be stuck in a room with Zack most of the day, and I'm afraid that I'll launch myself at him if we're in too confined of a space. Either to feel his lips against mine again or to rip his head off. It's tough to say at the moment.

"Any questions?"

David eyes both of us and smirks at Zack as the man in question shoves the last bit of his donut into his mouth.

"Did you bring me one?" he asks him, and of course Zack being a brown-noser nods his head. David opens the bag on his desk and smiles then turns his steely gaze toward me. "Since Zack made sure to grab my favorite donut, you are tasked with grabbing my favorite coffee downstairs. You have ten minutes."

"Seriously? I don't even know what you drink."

He shrugs and then begins to tap on the keyboard on his desk, pecking away as if he didn't just throw down the rope for a challenge. And I fucking hate to lose.

Gracefully standing from the chair, I move toward the door, but just as I'm about to exit I hear a snicker behind me. I instantly know that it's from David and when I turn around I see him gazing at his monitor with a grin on his face. But not before I noticed Zack's stare trained on my ass. He's lucky that I love my curves and I know what this dress particularly does for them.

I peek out of the door but I don't see David's secretary anywhere and I blow out a puff of air. When I worked in the coffee shop in college David never came to see me, saying that I shouldn't mix business with pleasure. So I'm walking into this challenge blindly. Until an idea forms in my mind.

Turning back into the room I look over at Zack and smile sweetly.

"Hey, Zack? I'm not quite sure how to find the employee coffee shop," I lie, because even though it wasn't shown during orientation, I noticed it on my way out the other day. But they don't know that. "Do you know how to get there from this level?"

"Yeah, I can take you."

"Thank you so much," I say, laying it on thick with a wide grin.

Of course David takes that moment to chime in, "You have seven minutes."

My smile wipes clean from my face as I turn to him and scowl, but he misses it as he digs into his drawer for something.

Zack follows me out of the room toward the bank of elevators.

"I know what you're doing. You're hoping I'll tell you what he likes to drink."

"Oh, I know you will," I whisper as we pass the empty receptionist desk for Fleming Coffee and make our way to the elevators.

"Yeah? How is that?" Zack naively asks as I press the down button for the elevator and the doors swoosh open before us.

I turn around and grab his tie as I walk backward into the car, pulling him in with me.

"Like this."

Tugging his tie, he falls against me as I press myself against the back of the cart. My hands hold each side of his face and I pull his head down to meet mine, sealing our lips together. Zack's arms immediately wrap around my waist, pulling my body closer. My tongue slips past my lips and tastes the top of Zack's begging for entrance, which he quickly allows.

I give myself a moment to take pleasure in the feeling of being in his arms, of feeling his mouth as he pours himself into the kiss, knowing that I've been craving this sensation since he left me Monday night.

But I only give myself that moment.

My hands glide away from his face and down his chest, convincing him that I want to feel his body. Instead, I grip both ends of his tie and tighten the knot against his collar with a yank.

"What the fuck?" he chokes out as I pull my face away from his, watching his face turn a ruddy shade of red.

"Tell me his favorite coffee."

"Or what?"

"Or I'll tighten this knot until you pass out, strip you naked, and leave you here."

"You wouldn't dare."

"Try me," I say as I tighten the knot just a tiny bit more.

"Fuck, fine," he chokes out, coughing as I loosen the tie enough for him to catch his breath. "He doesn't like coffee. He gets a chai tea latte. God, you're ruthless."

"I don't like to lose. But what kind of man runs a coffee chain and doesn't like coffee?"

Zack shrugs as we exit the elevator and he points me toward the small shop for employees while he opts to wait by the elevator bay. I place the order along with one for myself. I tap my fingers along the counter as I wait for the staff to finish the beverages, always cognizant of the time left in my challenge.

Drinks in hand I join Zack and he presses the button to call an elevator for us.

"You know, I could have gotten out of that tie hold."

I shrug my shoulders because I know he could have. He's much larger and stronger than I am and could have easily pulled my grasp free.

"You were hoping I'd kiss you again."

He remains silent as the doors open and we step inside. Zack presses the number for our floor and as the doors close, he turns toward me.

"You're right, I was."

He stalks toward me and I press myself against the back of the elevator again with the drinks in my hand held out away from me.

"And I get what I want, Blake. I know you want it too."

A steady hand delves into my hair, gripping it as he tilts my head back and melds our mouths together again. His taste is addictive, and I can see myself craving another hit.

The chime alerts us to our floor and Zack pulls away and walks out of the car without a backward glance. I don't have a moment to consider how I look or if time has elapsed in the challenge. All that I can think about in that very second is that Zack was totally right. I did want it too. Almost more than winning.

And that is definitely not in my plan.

I LEAVE BLAKE PONDERING OUR KISS IN THE elevator just as I bump into David in the lobby of his floor.

"What are you grinning for?"

"No reason," I insist as I pretend to fiddle with the button on my suit jacket when in reality I'm trying to cover the hardon Blake's kiss caused.

"Time's up, Blake," I hear David scold as she casually walks out of the elevator.

I watch her eyes grow in intensity as she stalks toward him and shoves the cup at his chest.

"Enjoy your drink," she tells him as she sways her hips more aggressively walking past both of us back toward David's office.

"Did she poison this?"

I turn my attention back to him, angry that his eyes stay trained to the back and forth movement of her backside. "You'll never know until it's too late. I guess that's a risk you're going to have to take."

Entranced he takes a sip and then looks down at the cup in shock.

"How did she get you to tell her?"

"How do you know that I did? Maybe she asked the barista."

"Fuck, don't leave her alone in my office for long. Who knows what she's capable of."

I don't reply as he heads down the hallway on the opposite side of the lobby and I make my way down the same path Blake had made moments ago, only to come to a halt when I find the door to David's office locked.

"Blake, open the door." I knock on the wooden entry three times, but I hear no reply. "Blake!" I shout more forcefully.

The door swings open wide with force, practically bouncing off the wall when it makes contact.

"Where is the list?" she seethes. If this had been a cartoon, smoke would be fuming from her ears.

"I don't know what you're talking about." Casually I lean on the doorframe crossing my arms against my chest.

"The task list, Zack. Somewhere in that teeny tiny brain of yours, I know that you understand what I'm talking about."

"Blake, nothing about me is teeny or tiny," I tell her with a half grin that has been known to land a few women in my bed a time or two.

Giving it a moment for her reaction to come forth, I'm surprised when she doesn't break her stare.

"Was that supposed to be funny?"

"No, just stating a fact."

"Well, it's irrelevant. I'd like to use my time today tackling this godforsaken list that David has created and then get to work on my campaign. So please, if you could act like an adult for five seconds, either give me the list or show me where it is located."

"Oh, are you referring to this list?" I ask as I pull the folded up piece of paper from my pocket. She tries to snatch it from my hand, but since I stand almost a foot taller, I hold it out of her grasp above her head.

"Dammit, Zack. Stop acting like a child."

I dangle the paper above her head and shake it as she tries to reach for it once more, chuckling every time her fingers skim across the bottom.

"I swear I will kick you in your most precious equipment if you do not hand me that freaking piece of paper," she dictates with such hostility that I actually fear for my balls. I bring the piece of paper down to her level, which she grabs with such a flurry that it leaves a paper cut along the palm of my hand.

"Shit," I shriek as I inspect the bleeding slash on my skin.

"Oops, sorry," Blake lies as she looks down to start reading through the list. "Hold on, he wants us to sharpen one hundred pencils so that only one-quarter of an inch of lead is visible." Looking up at me she asks, "Is he crazy? This is one of the most ridiculous things I've ever heard."

She's not wrong, but I want this contract and if David is going to make me play along, then so be it.

"How about you take fifty and I take fifty."

"Great, but do you have a ruler? I don't keep one in my purse you know," she spits back at me.

Shrugging my shoulders, I walk into the office and tell her, "You can get an app for one on your phone," as I take off my suit jacket, placing it on the chair next to her coat, and then roll up the sleeves of my dress shirt just above my elbows.

As I turn back around ready to make haste on this ridiculous assignment, I'm surprised to find Blake standing at the doorway with a stunned expression on her face and her cheeks a subtle shade of pink.

"What?"

"I. . .I didn't know that you had tattoos."

"Well, beautiful, we haven't seen each other in six years. I'm sure there is a lot that we don't know about each other."

Without a word, she walks toward me and I can see that she wants to admire the work of my full sleeve. Her fingers graze across my arm and an electric pulse shoots directly to my cock. The skulls, gears, and geometric shapes are all done in black shading, but throughout the piece are brightly colored scales and flowers.

"This is gorgeous," she tells me as she flips my arm around to see the other side. "Did it hurt?"

"Some parts like the elbow, but most of the time the adrenaline rush overpowers the pain."

"I'd love a tattoo, but I'm terrified of needles. I can't even stand to get my finger pricked."

In the course of two minutes, Blake and I are having the most civilized conversation I can remember. Since day one we've always been at each other's throats, but right now. . .right now, this moment is shedding light on the side of her that I always knew existed. The one she kept hidden away except to a select few and the side David always took advantage of.

As she continues to inspect the artwork, pointing out bits and pieces that she likes, I ask, "If you got a tattoo what would it be?"

"I don't know," she replies, looking up at me, but her hand never stops stroking my forearm. "I haven't really thought about it. Maybe something symbolizing strength or to remind me to keep moving forward."

Settling my hand on top of hers, I sandwich her delicate fingers between my palm and arm. "Well, if you ever settle on something I'd be happy to take you to my guy. I promise that it's nothing like getting a shot."

"Hmm. . . I'll think about it. Do you know where the supplies are?"

I'm so focused on the lushness of her mouth that I answer her with a confused expression.

"For the pencils and a few of the other tasks. Do you know where they keep the office supplies?"

"Oh. No, but I'm sure we can ask someone or wander around until we find them."

I watch her big hazel eyes transform before me with a gleam of interest.

"Race ya?" she asks, not waiting for a response as she dashes away from me and out of the office.

Oh, Blake, it is on.

Just as I bustle out of the office, I run smack dab into one of the associates. Spinning her around with my hands on her shoulders I ask her in a hurry, "Where is the supply room?"

Frazzled, the woman points merely down the hall toward the lobby and I run in that direction shouting a thank you. As I dart past each door I check the marker looking for one dictating that it's the supply closet.

Just as I glide across the marble floor of the small lobby I slam into Blake. Our chests are both heaving as we gasp for air. Simultaneously we turn our heads to the direction of my left and see the door labeled as the supply closet.

I reach out and tug on the knob but the door doesn't budge. It's locked up tight. I turn back to look at Blake and I'm surprised to see her smiling triumphantly.

"Oh, Joey," she calls out and the young man arrives swiftly at her beck and call. "Hi, do you think you could use your badge to let us into the supply closet? David has a few projects for us."

"Certainly, Ms. Holliday. I'd be happy to," he squeaks as he swipes his badge to unlock the door.

"Thanks," I grumble as Blake thanks Joey with a saccharine smile.

"Don't think you win that one, beautiful," I point out as I gather a few boxes of pencils. I move farther into the space from where Blake just came from to look for a sharpener like the one she has in her hand. Finally locating an extra one, I turn around to see Blake stepping out of the door.

"Oh, Zack, but I did." And just like that she closes the door to the supply closet with me locked inside.

Not even bothering to scream for help, I take a seat on a stack of printer paper and begin getting to work sharpening the pencils. I'm so lost in the project that I don't realize that two hours have passed until a few shouts outside of the door break me from my trance.

"Blake, you can't lock someone in the supply closet."

"Sure I can. If I could, I'd lock both of them in there."

"Come on, you don't mean that," I hear Thomas say to her. "I know that you and David have your differences, but Zack is a good guy. Put your egos aside and work together. That way when the Board sees your campaign, your hard work will shine through."

"You mean that?"

"Of course. You know that my money is on you."

Chiming in I shout, "I can hear you, you know."

Thomas replies quickly with a chuckle. "Of course I know that. You're not the first one to get locked in that closet, son. When my Nancy worked for me, she used to lock me in that room on a weekly basis just to make a point." Nancy is his deceased wife. I remember David telling me that she had passed away during our junior year in college.

"Do you miss her?"

"Not a day goes by where I don't miss her, but I'll meet her again soon. I wish everyone could find that sort of love in their life. Especially my grandson, but he has a lot of growing up left to do."

"You can say that again," I hear Blake mumble.

"Y'all can let me out now," I tell them.

The buzzer sounds as Thomas swipes his badge. He pushes the door open and gestures for me to exit.

"I'll leave you two. Forget the rest of David's list. I'll make sure he knows what I think about it," Thomas says as he pats my shoulder and then heads down the hall toward his office.

"Sorry," Blake grumbles as she looks down at the floor like a scolded child.

"Don't apologize," I tell her. "Had it been reversed you know that I absolutely would have locked you in here."

Finally, she looks up at me with that carefree smile I've only witnessed a handful of times and I can feel my heartbeat pound in my chest.

"So, since we have to be on our best behavior, do you want to go get lunch and toss around some ideas for the gala?"

My stomach growls at the mention of food. "Obviously, that sounds great to me. Mexican?"

"Perfect."

We walk together back to David's office to gather our things and I'm surprised to find him sitting at his desk when we return.

"Where are you going?" he questions as I help Blake into her coat.

"Thanks," Blake whispers, her hazel eyes peering up at me from beneath her lashes.

"We're going to lunch to discuss the gala. Are there any particulars you'd like to make sure are covered?"

David sits quietly for a moment and then shakes his head, most likely perplexed at the fact that Blake and I aren't bickering for once.

"Okay, I'll talk to you later."

We leave a silent David bewildered in his office as we join a crowd in the elevator and make our way out of the building. One of my favorite Mexican restaurants sits just a block over from the building.

A need of possession takes over me and I slip my hand out of my pocket and reach for Blake's. I'm surprised when she doesn't turn to punch me or question my motives, but I'm utterly shocked when she grips my hand just a touch tighter. We walk hand in hand down the sidewalk and across the street, neither of us pulling away from the other.

I bring us to a stop just outside of the restaurant as the crowd moves around us. Simultaneously we turn toward each other, our eyes locked as the world around us fades away. My hand reaches out, yearning to feel the soft skin of her cheek, but we're jostled free from our trance as a man pushes past us.

The moment is severed and we pull our hands away and walk into the restaurant, but for a small flash in time the devil and I called a truce and it was one of the most serene moments of my life.

As the host seats us at our table we both order a glass of water and glance over the menu.

"What's good here?"

"Everything," I joke. "I'm fond of their house special myself."

"Ooo, that sounds good. I'll take that." Placing her menu back on the table, she folds her hands together on top of the plastic covered paper and looks over to me. "So, do you have any ideas about the party?"

Not surprisingly I'm looking forward to this conversation. I have a much-kept secret that I enjoy event planning. I flourish under the stress and pressure and take pleasure in seeing the finished product.

"I do, actually. What about you?"

"I have a few, but I haven't been in the area long enough to know local vendors or venues. I guess I should start researching."

"Well, a little note about me, I enjoy planning events. I have an idea that I think would be unique and spectacular if you're open to it."

"I'm all ears," she says eagerly as she reaches into her bag and then opens a notebook onto the table, pencil ready in hand.

The laugh escapes my lips before I can think twice about it and I watch as her cheeks redden.

"What?"

"You're cute."

"Oh." Blake tucks her chin against her chest and her face flushes a bit more. I wish that I could pull my phone out to capture the moment.

"Anyway, I have a contact with the new aquarium that just opened. What do you think of renting the space for the evening? We can have guided tours, a sit down catered dinner, and create our own ball drop at midnight."

I watch as she stares at me blankly, her lids closing only a few times.

"I mean," I begin, "if you don't like it we can come up with something else."

"No," she rushes, "no, that's. . .that's a freaking amazing idea. I love it. Do you think we can pull it off? Can your contact get us the space?"

Tugging my phone from my pocket, I search through the contacts and land on Lily's number before pressing the call button.

"Hey, Lily, it's Zack. How are you? Good, good. So, I'm calling because I know we had already spoken about possibly booking the aquarium for New Year's Eve and I think that it's a go. Can you send me a quote for the rental? I need to get it approved before I can sign a contract. Oh, really? No cost?" I ask as I look up toward Blake's skeptical gaze. "Yes, I know that we're friends. Okay, okay. I give in. But we'll still pay the staff. Can you send me a list of the caterers? Thank you. Yeah, I'll tell Samantha to call you. Bye."

Ending the call, I place the phone back in my pocket and look up to see Blake practically leaning over the table eagerly waiting to hear more.

"So?"

"Oh. . . you mean the call?" I ask as if I don't know what she's referring to.

"Yes," she hisses.

"So, we have the venue free of cost, we only need to pay the servers and caterers, as well as the decorations. We can send Lily a list of the items we need for the dinner set up."

"Holy shit, I could kiss you right now."

Smirking, I lean on the table and bring my face close to hers. "I'm good with that."

Her eyes widen, but then she sits back in her chair while she looks around at the surrounding patrons of the restaurant.

"We have one more thing to discuss," she points out, grasping her pencil again and jotting some notes down in her notebook.

"What's that?"

"The theme."

"The theme," I repeat, leaning back in my chair and rubbing my hand along my scruff covered chin.

"Maybe we can come up with something different. The typical color schemes for New Year's parties are black and gold, right?"

"Right."

"What if we went with light blues and silver? It will be fresh and light. Maybe incorporate a lot of LED white lights since they take on almost a crisp whitish-blue hue."

"I like it. Let's do it."

Blake scribbles in her notebook as the server comes by to take our order and I gladly give our meal choice since she seems to be lost in her own world. I take a few sips of my water as she flips her page and begins doodling on her paper.

Just as the food arrives on the table Blake perks up in her seat with a level of enthusiasm I've never seen on her face before. She darts out of her chair and comes to stand beside me.

"Here, this is what I think we can do. I haven't seen the space, but I'm assuming the dinner will be served in a large open space with a stage and dance floor." As I nod, she continues, "What if we draped balloons in columns down from the ceiling to appear like air bubbles and the table centerpieces could be ferns that appear like sea kelp and coral?" Turning her drawing toward me, I take in her design. It's remarkable.

"This is great, Blake. I really like it. Where did you learn to draw like this?" I ask.

"You're not just messing with me? You like it?"

"I really do," I tell her as I hand her back the notebook. "You're very talented."

"Thanks," she replies, blushing again.

"So, where did you learn to draw like that?"

"Oh, I was just doodling. It's nothing special."

"Blake," I command, just as she's about to take a bite of her burrito. "Everything about you is special."

"Don't say things like that, Zack, or I'm likely to think that you actually like me."

"I can like to hate you."

Smiling she repeats, "I can like to hate you too."

RENEE HARLESS

I T IS A STRANGE FEELING TO WAKE UP IN THE morning expecting to feel one way but feeling the complete opposite. So many mornings in my past I have woken up feeling a sense of irritation at just the thought of Zack Nicholson's name. Knowing that I would be in his mere presence over a month ago would have sent my anger into a tailspin.

But three weeks ago something happened. Not just the kisses, they were perfect and way hotter than I could have imagined myself, but something more had taken place. We had gotten along. And when we spent a few hours working together and not following through with our typical bouts of spewing hateful things back and forth, he was actually someone I enjoyed talking to.

He was different from my friend Sofie; she understood business but not all of the creative processes that come with working in the marketing field. But Zack? Zack got it, and he understood my passion for certain things and I understood his.

So waking up expecting to fall into one emotional perspective but finding myself falling into another is tossing me for a whirlwind.

Because I like him.

When we aren't fighting, which still happened over the last few weeks, just not as frequently, I actually enjoy talking business with him and being around him.

I need to let Sofie into this new revelation because I'm so confused by my feelings that I'm not sure which way is up or down now. Am I supposed to be chummy with Zack? Is it okay to like him? What about the attraction we have? It's so strong that it is becoming harder and harder to ignore.

Completing my morning routine, I situate myself in the office to work on a few projects, including the Fleming campaign. My idea centers around focusing on the chain as a family owned and operated business, but what makes it unique is its employees. In our meeting with Thomas, he made it clear that the only thing that will hold someone back from working for his company is their actual willingness to work. He is recognized locally for employing persons with Down Syndrome and other challenges where other companies may have looked the other way. All he wants is that his customers are served with a smile and happy experience.

I'm not sure how he plans to ingrain that philosophy into David, because for every good measure that Thomas has, David equals the same on the other end of the spectrum. Besides their similar physical features, I would never have guessed that the two were relatives had I not known them previously.

"Good morning," Sofie greets as she springs through the door. She shakes off her coat which carries tiny flakes of snow on the shoulders.

"Uh oh? How's the weather?"

"Just a sprinkling, nothing to worry about."

"Whew, good. You know those forecasters. I think that they get a trip out of sending everyone out on wild goose chases when they aren't really expecting anything, but they stay silent when they know we're going to get hammered."

"I'd like to get hammered by a forecaster."

"What?"

"Sorry, I like the new meteorologist on the local station. He's sexy."

"Wow, okay. I'll have to check him out. Anyway, is there anything major on the agenda? I'll be in Charlottesville at the coffee shop on Broad and First from ten until two then I'll be at Seventh and Main from four until they close at nine."

"Gotcha." Sofie takes a seat at her desk and fiddles with her computer as she brings up her calendar. "I believe we just have a few progress calls this morning. I cleared out the rest of the time for you to work on projects."

"Thanks, Sof," I tell her as I bite my bottom lip and tap the end of my pen on my chin. "Hey, um. . ."

"What?" she asks curiously, peering up from her computer.

"I think I like Zack."

She nods, reminding me of a therapist you see on television as they absorb their patient's words.

"Okay, well I assumed that would happen at some point."

"No, Sofie. I mean I really like him. Like we've kissed and we're not fighting but actually getting along and I like to be around him. What am I going to do?"

"Hold on, back up. He kissed you?"

I nod and tell her that I may have kissed him too.

"So how many times have you kissed and why am I just now learning about this? You don't keep these things from your best friend."

"Three and it's not that I didn't want to tell you. I was just confused, and by telling you it made it all real, you know? Don't be mad."

"How was it? Please tell me that his kiss is just as hot as the rest of him."

"It was. . .it was everything, Sofie. Possessive, passionate. And, Sofie, he knows how to kiss really well. I've never been kissed like that." I can feel my face transform into a dreamy state, and as I look closer at Sofie her expression mimics mine.

"Wow," she whispers. "I think I'm going to need to change my panties after hearing that."

"Eww. Don't be gross."

Shrugging her shoulders, she doesn't apologize. Sofie has no filter.

"What should I do?"

"Bang him."

"Sofie!" I shout at her.

"What? Get him out of your system so you can go back to hating him. You don't want this attraction to knock you off your game of trying to get this contract with Fleming Coffee. Because, Blake, we need this. You need this."

"You're right. Maybe it's all a game anyway to get me distracted and lose focus. Now, come here and look over my idea for the campaign. I want to see if my timeframe will work."

I try to distract myself with the campaigns and projects, but in the back of my mind I know that I need to end whatever ceasefire Zack and I have silently agreed upon. This is my game to win, my world to rule, and he isn't going to uncrown this Queen.

Looping the ends of the string around my waist, I tie off the signature royal blue apron and turn to find Zack struggling to tie his.

"Want some help?" I chuckle as he gets more frustrated with the knot. I step over to him and swat his hands away as I take the ends and flawlessly perform the knot that we were instructed to use.

"There, perfect." I look up at him with my hands still on the strings and I find Zack gazing down at me with a longing expression. I want so badly to yank the knot and lose myself in his kiss, but I know that I need to stick to my plan.

I mock a cough as I step away from him and shove my hands into my pockets to keep myself from reaching out and touching him again.

"So. . ."

"How have you been?" he asks. We haven't worked together in three days, both of us dedicating time to some of our outside projects.

"Good. You?"

"Good."

The awkward silence drags on as we wait for instructions from the shop manager.

"They'll probably have us shadow another employee this morning so that we're up to speed for tonight at the busier shop."

"Let's hope so, because if they want me to start making specialty coffees right off the bat, then they're going to be sorely disappointed at my lack of skills," he states, shaking his head. I watch as the movement causes the waves of his hair to sway back and forth and I ache to run my hands through the locks.

Finally, the smiling manager makes her way over to us and explains that we'll each shadow one of their employees to learn the basics of working in the shop and then after the lunch rush we'll work to restock the items for the evening.

I'm introduced to Jose and he gives me some pointers on how their machines work and where everything is located. He lets out a sigh of relief when I tell him that I used to work in a coffee shop. Sparing a glance over toward Zack and the employee training him, I have to bite back my smile when he turns on the espresso machine and froth spews everywhere. Including all over himself.

What surprises me most is that instead of yelling at the employee for not telling him that he flipped the wrong switch and ruining his dress shirt and slacks, which David would have done, Zack tosses his head back and laughs. A full belly laugh that stirs something deep inside me that I don't want to spend time exploring.

The other employees and customers stare at him as if he's off his rocker, but I find myself smiling. Grabbing a towel from the sink, I toss it at Zack, and it smacks him in his face, ending his spell of laughter. He turns his face toward me and I shrug with the smile still plastered in place.

"Stop playing and get to work, Mr. Nicholson."

"Just having some fun, Ms. Holliday," he retorts and I shake my head as I go back to listening to Jose's instructions.

The shop works through the midday rush as one cohesive team, far from how the tiny coffee shop I worked at in college had been run. Zack even manages to make a few coffees without a disaster. I'm not sure how they taste since he never really follows the directions, but he hands each cup over with one of his sexy smiles that no woman or man complains.

Before we're scheduled to leave, the manager points us in the direction of the stockroom and Zack and I spend the hour sorting and stacking cups, lids, cardboard carriers, and bags.

"You did well today, Zack. I'm impressed that you didn't poison anyone and everyone left happy," I tell him as we walk into the small breakroom to remove our aprons and gather our things.

"Thanks. I may have actually had some fun today," he says as he returns my smile. As he removes his apron, we both notice the brown coffee stains splattered across his light blue dress shirt. How he managed to stain it beneath the apron, I'll never know. I wore all black today knowing that coffee and light-colored clothing never went well together.

"Shit," he murmurs as his strong hands swipe through his hair leaving it in an unruly mess.

"Do you have another shirt in your car? I mean it's not really a big deal, it is just going to get covered in more coffee this evening, I'm sure."

"I know you're right, but it's going to distract me the rest of the day. And I don't have anything else with me."

My brows furrow together as I try to come up with a solution, but I've got nothing.

"Don't you live close by? You could just run home and change then meet me at the other shop this evening."

Nodding his head, he asks, "What are you going to do? I thought we could use the time to talk about the gala."

"It's no problem. I can probably use the time to get some Christmas shopping done since it's right around the corner. Plus side of being my own boss."

"What's it like, running your own business?"

Sliding my arms into my coat and wrapping my scarf around my neck I contemplate my answer.

"It's stressful and chaotic, but I wouldn't want it any other way. It's a powerful feeling knowing that you get to make all of the decisions. Everything rests on your shoulders, you know? And since Sofie is my employee, her livelihood rests on my shoulders too. But to be twenty-eight and own my own business was not something I had ever imagined. Now, I wouldn't do anything else."

"Wow, you make it sound both terrifying and exhilarating."

"That's exactly it," I tell him as we walk out of the shop to our cars parked across the street. "It's this beautiful mesh of both of those things."

Stopping beside my compact car, I notice a few snowflakes floating down from the clouds. A few smatter on my cheeks and Zack reaches out to swipe at the one that lands on the tip of my nose.

"Thanks. I'll see ya this evening. Bring your A-game."

"Beautiful, I always bring my A-game. I'll just make sure to bring a change of clothes too," he jokes, both of us chuckling as we get into our separate cars.

He pulls out and tosses a wave in the air as he leaves the parking lot. Waiting for my car to heat up, I open my planner and laptop and opt to do some work in my car for a little bit to kill some time.

About half an hour later I end a phone call with the insurance company fighting with me over my dad's injury. I'm angry and dismayed at the lengths they're going to fighting me on this. If I had the money, I'd hire another attorney, a better one than before.

My cell phone buzzes and I see a message from Zack asking if I am still at the mall. I reply that I've been working and will be heading that way. He offers to join me and I figure, why not? He'd probably be a good punching bag right now since I can't go after the insurance company.

Asshole #1: Meet you there in ten.

Me: Sounds good. I'll meet you at the food court.

Just messaging about food makes my stomach rumble in hunger and I think that a big slice of pizza is exactly what I need.

"SO, WHO ALL DO YOU NEED TO SHOP for?" I ask Blake as we set our plates of pizza on a small table in the center of the food court.

"Oh. Just Sofie and my dad. You?"

"Well, typically just my parents, but Samantha and I are planning a surprise Christmas and anniversary party for my parents, so I'll probably need to pick up something for all twenty-some people coming in. Maybe you can help me."

Blake nods as she takes a huge bite of her pizza.

"How long have they been married?"

"Thirty years. They didn't wait too long to have me, obviously."

"Wow. Nowadays it's rare to hear of people staying married longer than three years. They must really love each other."

"They do, it's almost sickening. While I was having my house renovated this past year I stayed with them and let me tell you something. It may sound sweet, but watching your parents walk out of their bedroom with silly smiles on their faces every morning is enough to make you vomit in your mouth."

"Oh, it can't be that bad. And consider yourself lucky, after my mom left, my dad never dated around. I've never actually seen him with a woman until Maggie."

A few weeks ago Blake had spoken to me about the difficulties of being at home with her disabled father and trying to work at the same time. She described how challenging it was for her to leave her dream job and travel back to a place she had tried so hard to forget. I tried to talk to her about our years at college to pinpoint exactly where she and I had gone wrong, but she shot down my attempt and changed the subject.

"Do you think your dad and Maggie have something going on?" I ask her, but she shakes her head.

"I don't think so. My dad is so stubborn and he really puts Maggie through some trials. Just the other day he pretended to not feel well so he could skip therapy and watch a game on TV he had recorded the night before. By the time Maggie had caught on her time was up. But she put him through his paces the next day."

"They kind of sound like us," I mention and watch as Blake's doe eyes widen further.

"I guess so," she whispers and then turns her attention to the Christmas scene set up at the other end of the food court where Santa waits to greet some children.

The rest of our lunch is eaten in silence, Blake's eyes trained to the scene over my shoulder. With her lost in her own world, I keep my gaze locked on her. Even with her long hair pulled back off her face into a ponytail and her makeup a bit smudged from our work at the coffee shop, I remember seeing her when I strolled into the food court not long ago and thought that she was one of the most naturally stunning women I had ever set my eyes upon. It's the same feeling I had that first day I had walked into our intro to marketing class and watched her take the seat in front of me. Blake had glided into the room, head down, notebooks pressed against her chest, but she and I had locked eyes as she turned to take her seat. I had been hooked from that moment on.

Not much has seemed to change apparently, except our reasoning to hate each other. I can barely remember the reason I had fought her all those years ago and I wonder if she remembers her argument. Sometimes I consider asking, but I think again. We've been getting along well the past few weeks and I'm afraid to stir things up and evoke those emotions again.

"Do I have pizza sauce on my face? You're staring at me."

"You're beautiful."

That sweet flush that I'm becoming addicted to grows on her cheeks and I wish I could feel that same flush grow beneath the palm of my hand.

"You're crazy, I look like shit right now," Blake protests as she swipes her hand down the length of her hair pulled tight against her head.

"Blake, you could be wearing a trash bag and you would still be gorgeous. Now, come help me grab some gifts for my cousins that I haven't seen since they were barely walking."

"How old are they now?" she asks, gathering our plates and dumping them in the trash.

"Thirteen, fourteen, and two sixteen-year-olds."

She raises her wrist to check the time on her watch and then gasps in alarm.

"Zack, we only have two hours to shop for them! That is not enough time." Yanking my arm, she drags me toward a bookstore at the other end of the mall mumbling that men don't know anything.

An hour and a half later I stand outside a trendy shop where Blake had seen something that caught her eye for Sofie, but even with my arms weighted down with several bags of gifts for my family, I spot something across the way that I absolutely need to have. Not for me, but for Blake.

"Hey, all set. I think we tackled everyone. That's a relief."

"Blake," I call out to her in the midst of her rambling, "do you have a dress for the gala?"

"Um, well, no. But I'm just going to wear a black dress that I have in my closet."

"No, you're not," I tell her as I start walking toward the shop, my mind set on Blake wearing this gown.

"Where are you going?" she shouts and then rushes to catch up to me just as I ask one of the assistants for a particular dress in the window in Blake's size. Luckily the woman takes a good guess and goes to the mannequin and strips it bare.

"This is actually the only one we have and it just happens to be in her size," she tells me and Blake looks at us in confusion.

"Whose size?"

"Yours," I explain as I hand the woman my credit card to purchase and bag up the gown.

Hands fisted at her side Blake raises her voice as she asks, "How do you know my size?"

"He didn't. I did," the woman ringing up the gown admits. "That's part of my job, and I am never wrong." The sleek woman looks over to Blake and pins her with a glare silently requesting Blake to challenge her. "Would you like to try it on before you leave?"

"No, that's okay. If it doesn't fit it's not my waste of money."

"It will fit and will look amazing on you," she tells Blake and then looks back at me as she hands me my credit card and hangs the dress in a custom garment bag. "Thank you very much for your purchase today. Happy Holidays."

"You as well."

Once we step out of the store, Blake spins around and levels me with her glare. "Why would you do that? Now I owe you a gift."

"You don't owe me anything, beautiful. My gift will be seeing you wear it. Believe me."

We engage in a staring contest, neither of us budging, and just when I'm afraid I'm going to lose and give in to allowing Blake to grab a gift for me, she averts her gaze and drops her shoulders.

"Fine, you win. No gift. And thank you, the dress really is remarkable."

Holding my hand to my chest, I fake shock at her compliment.

"Am I having a heart attack? Did you actually concede at something and praise my gift?"

Swatting my shoulder, she giggles saying, "Yeah, don't let it go to your head. This will be the only time it happens."

"Come on, I believe there is more manual labor for us this evening."

"Great," she groans as we head back to our cars to load our bags and head to the second coffee shop.

The moment we walk into the second coffee shop we are thrust into organized chaos. I even notice Blake take a step back toward the exit as we realize the madness we're about to join.

"I'll tell Thomas and David if you leave."

Sneering at me Blake recoils, "You wouldn't dare."

"Wouldn't I?" I inquire as I tug off my jacket and toss it over my arm ready to get to work.

Just as I'm walking toward the counter I hear her growl, "I hate you again."

"I know."

I wait for Blake to join me before I introduce us to the manager who immediately tosses a few aprons our way and asks us to get to work. Blake and I follow her to the small breakroom and lock our stuff in one of the free cubbies.

Back out front, Blake and I look around the mass of people loitering about the shop and gaze around in amazement.

"Hi!" a chipper teenager says as she steps in front of us. "You must be Zack and Blake. Mr. Fleming called and said you'd be here tonight." She barely takes a breath, not letting us return her welcome. "One of you has experience right?"

"That's me," Blake replies, raising her hand like we are back in class at college.

"Great!" the teen chirps. "We have you on station two duty. Zack, you're on cleaning duty."

I breathe out a sigh of relief knowing I won't have to make drinks for any customers and I'm actually surprised to see the look of excitement in her eyes. If there is anyone that can rise to the occasion, it's Blake.

Surprisingly enough, the evening passes quickly and I'm caught off guard when the girl from earlier prances over to the door and locks it then flips the sign to closed.

"Great work, everyone."

I spent the entire evening sweeping floors, emptying the trash, and restocking supplies for the other employees. I haven't been on my feet that long in a very long time so I'm astonished to find that I'm energized and ready to tackle anything. Like the girl standing on the other side of the counter wiping down her mess. Her hair is standing off kilter on her head, loose strands fall in soft wisps around her face, but her smile mirrors mine – vast and brilliant.

Smacking my hands on the counter Blake startles and then laughs when she finds me standing in front of her. Gathering my apron from around my neck and body I lay the material on the counter and ask Blake if she's ready to go. She nods enthusiastically.

"Thanks for letting us help out today," I tell the manager as she steps over to count down the cash registers. "I hope that we didn't get in the way too much."

"Not at all," she replies. "If you all ever want to come back we'd have you with open arms. It was a pleasure to meet both of you. You both be careful getting home tonight. Heck of a storm outside."

"You have a great night as well," Blake tells her as she sidles up next to me, her body so close that I can instantly feel the heat coming off of her skin.

Blake takes the lead and I follow her to the front door where the teen from earlier unlocks the knob to let us out. As I'm giving my thanks, I run smack into the back of Blake, practically tripping over her and knocking us both to the ground.

I'm not looking at my surroundings as I place both of my hands on her shoulders to steady her, loving how her slim figure fits in my palms.

A screeching noise brings my attention to the road before us and that's when I realize why Blake had stopped. Layer upon layer of fresh powdery snow dwells on the streets and sidewalks. The car that had beckoned my attention is sliding into another vehicle parked on the road, directly in front of us.

"It's going to take me forever to get home."

Something dominant and protective takes shape inside my gut, an instinct to keep this woman safe at all costs begins to swell up and make itself known.

"You're not driving in this."

With enough fire in her eyes to melt the icy precipitation around us Blake pins her gaze on me, luckily I'm immune to her devilish glare.

"Excuse me?"

"You're not driving in this. No one should be, the roads weren't even prepped ahead of time."

"I know how to drive in the snow, Zack."

Holding up my palms in the air as an act of surrender I try to explain myself.

"It's not that you don't, Blake. But obviously, not everyone else does." I gesture to the car that has collided with the other across the way. "You have a thirty-minute drive home from here on a good day, tonight would take you hours if you just crept by. And I'm sure if we asked your father, he would be furious that you're even considering driving home."

Her demeanor changes and her body deflates at my observation.

"You're right. Why'd you have to bring my father into this?"

"Because he cares about you and I know that I don't want anyone I care about driving in this."

"It sounds like you care about me a lot?" she asks with an odd mixture of skepticism and hope threading through her words.

It's the hope that leaves me floundering.

"I. . .uh . . .care about you. As a person. I mean. . ."

And as quickly as it appeared, it disappears from her eyes as she turns away from me to look back at the road. "I know what you mean. I guess I should see if there are any hotels close by." Grabbing her phone from her bag, she begins to search the area.

"You don't need a hotel; you can stay with me for the night. I don't live far."

"I'm not sure I want to go to your harem lair."

"Besides my family, you would be the first female to set foot in my house."

"Really?" Her phone forgotten, she looks up at me in surprise.

Nodding my head, a cold, blustery wind sweeps around us and Blake instinctively steps closer to me to shield herself from the biting air. I pull her close and wrap my arms around her as she buries her face against my chest, nuzzling against me to stay warm.

"My car is all-wheel drive so we should be fine to make it to my house. If you're okay with that."

"Yeah, it's fine," she murmurs, slipping her arms underneath my jacket and around my waist.

We walk like this down the block to where our cars are parked, neither of us pulling away from the hold we have on the other. Something about this feels different, feels right. And I physically ache when I have to push her away and place her onto the passenger seat.

The interior of the car buzzes and sparks from the density of our attraction. I am almost sure that if I light a match, the vehicle will go up in flames.

I wait for the car's interior to heat up, grateful that we were able to park in a covered deck saving me from having to sweep snow from my windshield. I'm actually nervous to see how Blake reacts to my house. I've never brought anyone outside of family into my home, not even David.

Just as the nerves begin to unsettle me and I contemplate telling Blake that I'll take her to a hotel instead, a soft warm hand glides against mine, the delicate fingers feeling so perfect as they're interlaced against the larger ones of my own.

She instantly calms me and I look intently at her as she matches my stare. Hazel to green. And if it isn't for the car alarm sounding off from across the lot causing us to startle and break apart, I'm almost certain I would have leaned forward to kiss her.

I can see myself falling for her; the hate I felt for so many years evaporating before my eyes giving way to a violent attraction. But the most unsettling part is what the angel with the dark wings plans to do with my heart in the palm of her hand.

RENEE HARLESS

CHAPTER five

ZACK DRIVES US SLOWLY OUT OF THE CITY toward a quaint neighborhood mixed with various styles of homes, nothing cookie-cutter about it. But as I'm taking in each home nothing about them screams "Zack" to me. Not until he pulls off onto a gravel path and his headlights showcase a beautiful farmhouse atop a hill.

Not that Zack looks like a farmer, but it's more that both he and the house possess a certain classic quality and charm. I doubt he has ever encountered a person he couldn't sweep off their feet with his charisma. Well, maybe just me, but even now I'm having a hard time reconciling the Zack I knew in college with the Zack that is quickly worming his way into my heart.

"Is this your place?" I ask him while he maneuvers the vehicle into the attached garage.

"I certainly hope so. Otherwise, the owners are about to get one heck of a surprise."

Instinctively my arm reaches out and I smack his shoulder saying, "Don't be a jerk," but as I'm pulling away, he grips my retreating hand in his.

My breath leaves my lungs at the contact in a gasp. He interlaces our fingers but keeps our hands hanging in the air.

"If you don't like the inside please don't tell me. I'm not sure my ego could take it."

A puff of air escapes my mouth in a quick laugh. "I don't think your ego has anything to worry about."

"Strangely enough I actually care what you may think."

"Why?"

"I don't know," he whispers, and it's at that moment that I realize we've begun leaning toward each other in the car. Only a small sliver of space remains between us.

My gaze falls to his full mouth and I am transfixed, completely unable to look away as his tongue slips out and wets his lips.

"Don't look at me like that, Blake."

"Like what?" I innocently inquire.

"Like you want me to take you right here in the middle of my garage," he growls, and a vein in his neck throbs out of his skin, his self-control barely hanging by a loose thread.

Without a second thought I reply, "Maybe I do."

"Fuck," he bellows as he pulls away and throws his head back against his headrest looking toward the roof of the car. I immediately miss the heat from his touch.

The need to apologize sits on the tip of my tongue, but I think better of it. Because I'm not sorry. Because I want to explore this attraction I have for Zack. Because I want to feel again, feel something other than stress and fear, feel myself let go.

"You deserve better than to be taken in a car, Blake. You deserve to be worshipped for hours."

Zack doesn't give me a moment to counter as he opens the door to his vehicle and exits, rounding the hood to open my door.

"Thanks."

Guiding me through the entrance from the garage, we step directly into a kitchen that opens up to a large living room. Everything that I see is warm and inviting and the space looks lived in. I hate walking into someone's home and feeling as if I shouldn't touch anything. That's how it is whenever I would go with Sofie to visit her parents at their mansion. But Zack's house is the opposite. I can see myself sipping some hot chocolate in the chair by the fireplace looking through the window at the wintery scene outside.

"Can I take your coat?"

"Oh," I say, shaking my head remembering where I am. "Thanks. This space is gorgeous, Zack. I really like it. Can you give me a tour?"

"Sure, but let's get some food started. Are you as hungry as I am?"

"Famished."

"I have a few steaks I picked up at the store this morning. Unless. . .are you a vegetarian?"

"No, I'm not. Meat sounds good."

And I wish that the floor would open up and swallow me whole. It's instances like this that I wish I wasn't so pale because I can feel the heat building on my cheeks. Obviously, Zack takes my words the way I didn't intend because he chokes back a cough.

"Um . . . can I use your bathroom?"

"Sure, it's around that corner on the left."

I find the powder room easily and take a second to freshen up by letting my hair down and swiping some cold water under my eyes to take away some of the smudged makeup. I wish that I had a change of clothes here, but I'll have to make do with what I have on.

Opening the door, I'm surprised to find Zack standing there with one hand poised to knock and the other holding a stack of folded clothes.

"I thought you might like to change. These are some of Samantha's clothes for when she comes to stay. I don't think she'd mind you borrowing them."

"Wow, I was just thinking that I'd like something else to put on. Thank you. Samantha is a bit smaller than me, but hopefully I can make these work."

"I've started the steaks; you have about fifteen minutes before they're ready."

"Oh, do you have a shower I could pop into?"

"Sure, let me show you to the guest bath."

I follow behind Zack, and as he takes me down the hall, I try not to admire the way his shirt stretches along his back muscles. Or the way his suit pants curve around his magnificent ass.

Maybe Sofie is right and I just need to get him out of my system, because right now, having sex with Zack is all that's on my mind.

He shows me the door to the bathroom and points out the toiletries I can select from, most of them being Samantha's. Not having siblings or being close to any relatives, I admire the relationship Zack has with his cousin.

"I'll be right out," I tell him as I slip into the bathroom and immediately turn the shower faucet on as hot as it will go.

I'm only in the steaming room for a few minutes, but I feel like a new woman as I exit the guest room and make my way down the hall toward the kitchen. Samantha's sweatpants mold themselves to my ass and her shirt is snug around my breasts, but neither are uncomfortable. And to be honest, I'd still wear them even if they were because removing the clothes I had spent all day in was probably one of the most exhilarating experiences I've had today. It's like that feeling you get when you arrive home after a long day at work and rip your bra off the moment you walk through the door.

"Wow, that smells delicious," I call out as I enter the kitchen but stop dead in my tracks when I witness Zack leaned against the counter wearing basketball shorts. Only basketball shorts, hung so low on his hips that I can make out two dimples just above his bottom.

I never knew that someone could actually drool at the same time that their mouth dries out completely, but it happens to me at that moment.

"Hey, you were quicker than I thought you'd be." He smirks, standing up straight to face me and place his phone on the counter of his kitchen island.

"Shirt," I call out like a weirdo that's never seen a man without a shirt on. It's only happened a handful of times, but still, nothing compares to Zack's bare chest before me. He's toned with a chiseled eight-pack giving way to the V-line on his hips that point like an arrow to the package tucked away in his shorts.

"Oh, sorry," he apologizes as he runs his hands across his stomach. "I had run a load of laundry this morning, so I tossed them in the dryer just now. Does my bare chest bother you, Blake?" he asks seductively.

Attempting to cover up my bizarre behavior I place a hand on my hip and flick my other in the air brushing away something invisible. "Pssh, no. I've seen tons of chests. So many that I can't even keep count."

He cocks one of those dark eyebrows at me and nods in disbelief. "Sure. If you want to take a seat in one of the stools, dinner will be ready in a second. I'll grab a shirt so that I don't distract you."

"You won't distract me," I argue.

"Good. I don't usually wear anything when I'm home, so you're lucky I put pants on."

Yeah, lucky me.

"Wow, it's really coming down out there," I point out as he plates our dinner. "I wonder if we need to reschedule the catering meeting tomorrow."

"We can play it by ear. Did you call your dad and let him know where you are? I wouldn't want him to worry."

"I sent him, Sofie, and Maggie a message when I was getting dressed." Cutting into the steak, I take a hearty bite and close my eyes in ecstasy.

"That good, huh?"

"This is amazing. I've never tasted anything so perfect before."

"Neither have I," Zack replies with his eyes glued to me. I squirm under his gaze and continue to eat bits and pieces of the meal, but my appetite has suddenly fallen to the wayside. There is something else that I'm hungry for, and it's tall, muscled, and within an arm's reach.

Giving myself a mental pep talk, I advise myself to be direct and straightforward with Zack and tell him what I want.

"Zack, I-," I begin but I'm interrupted when he asks, "Are you done?"

I nod and I'm about to take the chance to speak again but the words are stolen from my mouth as Zack slides his hands into my hair and seals our lips together. Our mouths crash and teeth clink as we both attempt to take command of the kiss. I feel my body igniting in flames as our tongues duel and the sensuous touch of his thumbs caress the upper bones of my cheeks.

"Are you sure that you want this with me? Because if you say yes then there is no going back, Blake. Once I have a taste of you, I won't be able to stop."

I'm love drunk and at a loss for words, so I do the one thing I know that will prove to him how much I want him. Climbing down from my stool I move onto his and wrap my legs around his waist, then mimic his move and meld our lips together once more. Zack drops his hands from my hair and slides them down to grip my ass as one of my hands snakes into his thick hair to see if it really is as luxurious as it looks. I'm not disappointed.

I yank at the strands and I'm immediately met with a growl from his throat that I feel vibrate all the way down to the apex of my thighs. And not to be outdone, Zack returns my tug with a smack on my ass. Except instead of a yelp I moan into his mouth.

"Dirty girl," he tells me just before I find myself falling onto a soft surface. I hadn't even realized that we had been moving, I was too lost in our kiss, too lost in the desire.

"Are you sure that you want this, Zack? Because this won't change anything," I repeat his question. But the lie burns as it passes through my lips and I hate it. Because whether I like it or not, things have already changed between us.

Zack doesn't respond. Instead he grinds his erection against my aching center letting me know in no other terms that he wants me as much as I want him.

"That answer your question?"

"Yep," I say, reaching up to grip the armrest beside my head at the same time Zack leans forward and leaves a trail of kisses along my jaw down to my shoulder, each peck boiling my blood beneath my skin.

"Good. Now let me worship you."

Old insecurities begin to fester and grow deep inside of me begging to take over and be set free, but I push them aside. It's nothing Zack hasn't seen before. Hell, he's the reason I have many of these insecurities. He's seen that I have a birthmark on my lower hip strangely in the shape of California and that there are a few lines and stretch marks around my ass from where I worked hard to lose the Freshman fifteen. I can't let those thoughts flourish. I want this moment more than my last breath. And if he's dissatisfied with how my body looks now, then it is his loss.

Zack lifts the edge of my T-shirt, tossing it haphazardly across the room, and then slowly removes my borrowed sweatpants, leaving me in my lace bra and panties. I'm overwhelmed by the look of awe on his face. It's as if he's seeing me for the first time and can't believe he's been so lucky. Or maybe that is just wishful thinking on my part.

"Fuck, you're beautiful." His gaze skims over my body, heating every inch of my skin wherever his eyes land. "I knew you would be, but damn," Zack claims as his hands slide up my thighs, hips, and stomach before landing on my breasts.

I'm about to reply with some sort of snarky comment, but all thoughts leave my mind as he tugs down the cups of my bra, exposing my breasts to him. His strong hands palm the mounds of flesh, his attention never wavering as he works my nipples into hard peaks. My free hand searches for his forearm in the softly lit room and then slides up to rest on his muscled bicep. Zack's eyes lock on mine as I gently squeeze the muscles of his arm and we maintain that contact as he leans forward and swirls his tongue around one of the pert buds on my breast before closing his lips around it.

I want to shut my eyes to give into the sensation but I can't look away from Zack's stare. He's commanding me to maintain the connection without a single word. He switches his movements to my other breast and I can feel my hips beginning to rock in place. Slow, subtle movements as I seek friction against my most sensitive spot. He must recognize my need because at the same time he sucks at my nipple Zack rocks his erection against my panty-covered sex.

"Oh, fuck," I cry out, tossing my head back as waves of pleasure roll through me, my back arches and I thrust my breast farther into Zack's mouth.

"You taste exactly how I imagined. So sweet," he points out. The cold air caresses my breast as Zack moves to trail kisses down my stomach, leaving no space not tasted by his lips and tongue.

"What if I want to taste you?"

Sitting back onto his heels Zack scoops the edges of my panties into his fists and tugs them down and over my ankles. I want to clench my thighs together, rarely having exposed myself to a man this way before, but his hands settle on my knees and push my legs wider apart.

I can see the ravenous fire in his eyes and he licks his lips as if my sex is his life source and he's a dying man in the desert.

"You can taste me later. I've waited ten years to have you like this, Blake. Let me have you."

Ten years? I begin to question but then I'm suddenly lost and drifting away into rapture as his mouth lands on my center. I lose all train of thought and let myself relish in the sensations.

Pulling back, Zack looks up from between my legs in awe. "Fucking hell, I knew you would be perfect. I'm not sure I'm going to be able to stop." His eyes travel back down to where he slides his fingers back and forth through my slick folds spreading my essence around my bare mound. His thumb begins to press small circles around my clit as his tongue pulses in and out of my slit.

I'm not usually one to come when a man feasts on me in this way, my embarrassment always at the forefront of my mind, or maybe it was because David was a selfish lover. But Zack has my body quivering under his ministrations far quicker than I would have ever thought possible.

"Let yourself go, beautiful," he demands, the speed of his actions intensifying.

"Shit," I moan out in a whisper, my back arching and my toes curling from the force of the orgasm that has caught me by surprise.

Zack slows his movements, allowing me to drift back from my climax and fall into a sated state.

My breathing fills the room coming in fast pants and I rest a hand on my chest to feel the rapid beats of my heart that I had believed had all but been covered in cobwebs at this point.

"Holy cow, I've never felt anything like that before," I explain, opening my eyes to find Zack's intense stare pouring into me, igniting the fire that should have fizzled out after the orgasm of epic proportions that I just had.

"I'm not done with you."

Zack steps away from the couch just as I ask, "What?" and lifts me into his arms. I should feel mortified that my lower region is exposed and hanging freely in the air while my breasts are pressed upward in their hold from my bra. But instead of that emotion streaming through me, all I feel is a sense of safety in Zack's arms. And the physical press of his cock on my lower back. That's the feeling that is most evident.

He carries me down the hall toward a room at the end with double doors. Continuing to hold me with one strong arm, he twists the knob with his other hand and then flicks on a lamp resting on the top of a long dresser beside the door.

The curious person in me wants to take a moment to look around the space and learn more about this mysterious man that I have seemed to have pegged incorrectly, but instead, I'm enthralled with the way his eyes turn from light green to a dark hunter shade as we walk closer to the bed.

Placing me in the center of his king-size bed, Zack wastes no time shucking off his shorts and reaching into his nightstand to open a new box of condoms and snatches out a sleeve, tearing one open and sliding the latex down his shaft. My mouth hangs open in awe at the imposing length of his cock. Long and thick, the tip bobs past his belly button as it stands at full mast. If Michelangelo needed inspiration for a sculpture, I would nominate Zack every time. Every muscle on his body is defined and hard. He's a chiseled work of art that I get to have to myself for one night.

I gulp audibly and Zack chuckles. "You like?"

"It's. . .intimidating."

He places one knee on the bed and then the other knee follows as he crawls over my body and rests his hips on top of mine. One of his hands softly strokes my face and combs through my hair.

"I'll be gentle. How long has it been?"

"Longer than it should be."

"That's a real shame. Your body should be treasured."

'Yeah. . .well, I haven't found anyone worth sharing it with."

Bending down Zack presses his lips against mine and his tongue seeks entrance into my mouth which I eagerly accept. Ever since that first kiss in the hallway of the bar I've become addicted to his taste, praying for it every time he's in my presence.

But I just want the kiss. It has nothing to do with Zack. Atleast, I keep telling myself this.

"I'm honored," he whispers against my mouth, his hips rocking against my soaked center, coating himself in my heat.

"You should be," I sassily reply.

"Watch your mouth or we'll see what it can really do. I'm dying to see my cock slide between your plump lips."

My body shivers as his hand skates down the side of my body, across my hips, down my thigh, only to grip it tightly and bend my leg in the air. Zack rocks against me one more time before the tip of his erection poised at my entrance then slips inside. A few short thrusts in and out and then Zack buries himself to the hilt.

"Oh, God," I cry out at the sharp bite of pain that gives way to a feeling of fullness.

"Zack," he growls as he slips his cock out of my sex and then glides back in. "Not God. Zack. I want to hear you cry my name out in pleasure."

The speed and intensity increase and I reach out to grip the covers at my sides at the same time he lifts both of my legs and spreads them wide.

A hiss flees from his lips as he tosses his head back. "Fuck. You. Feel. Good," he punctuates with each maniacal thrust.

I'm entranced watching him, watching the beads of sweat drip down his chest, watching the way his fingers grip tighter around my thighs, watching the way he loses each ounce of control he works so hard to maintain. It's chaotic, and frenzied, and utterly captivating.

"Touch yourself, Blake," he commands. I hesitate for a moment. I've never touched myself during sex, only when I'm alone in my room needing to relieve stress, but the way Zack demands to see me touch myself is single-handedly one of the most erotic moments of my life.

I release my grip on the sheet and reach across my body to find the small bundle of nerves known to throw me over the edge quickly. The sound of slick skin smacking against each other and heavy pants from myself and Zack echo in the room as I locate my sensitive bud.

I increase the pressure of my fingers as I lose myself in the rush to find my release at the same time Zack thrusts faster and harder. If I knew it was physically possible, I'd be certain Zack is going to break me in half at the force in which he's burying himself inside my body. Like he wants to leave a part of himself etched in me to remember him for a lifetime.

Like I could ever forget after tonight. As his body jerks at the same time as mine everything shifts around us. The colors seem brighter and the world more clear. We've launched ourselves from purgatory into a heavenly kaleidoscope of sensations.

After a minute Zack shifts himself and pulls me into his arms as his cock slips free from between my legs and I instantly miss the feeling of him buried inside me.

"Sorry, I'll be more gentle next time," he explains as he curls my body against his.

"Next time?"

His hand reaches up and strokes the ends of my hair as I settle against his chest, ignoring the feeling of rightness at resting in his arms.

"Oh yeah. I'm definitely not through with you yet. I've only had a taste. I want the entire buffet. Just give me like five minutes to recoup."

"So, we're going to need that entire sleeve you pulled out?" I joke as he turns me onto my back, pressing his body against mine. His laugh is all of the answer I need.

"Oh, beautiful. We're going to need the entire box. And it's a jumbo pack."

IT WAS SURREAL LAYING HERE IN MY BED with Blake snuggled tightly against me. Something I had dreamt of so many times when we were in college together. The agony of knowing she was sleeping across the hall in David's room was like twisting the knife that had been fully lodged in my chest. She'd wrap her delicate hands around the end of the blade and turn it, collecting every ounce of my blood until she wrung me dry.

If you had asked me two months ago, hell, three weeks ago if I would find myself lying here with Blake in my arms after exploring every inch and curve of her delectable body I would have called you a fool. But I'm the fool. I'm already caught up in her, wanting more than just the one night. A night that occurred solely by happenstance. Had the snow not kept her from going home she wouldn't be here right now, and I wouldn't have had the opportunity of taking advantage of our snowed-instate.

"You are thinking very very hard over there."

I tilt my head to find Blake's chin perched on her hands which rest on my chest. Her head bobs with every breath I take and the soft flutter of her hair tickles my stomach.

"It's nothing. Just going to a place in my head where I shouldn't be."

"What place is that?" she asks curiously.

Nervously I stroke my hand through my hair debating on telling her how much I ached to be with her in college. How it was torture watching David treat their relationship like it was nothing.

Just as I make the decision to tell her some of what had been playing back in my head, her phone rings from the nightstand. We had snuck back into the kitchen early in the morning when our stomachs protested in hunger.

"Hey, Sofie. Yeah, it's still on my schedule. We can probably meet them this afternoon if they're still up for it. I just need to run home and grab a change of clothing. Are the roads any better? No, Sofie. Sofie. Sofie! I'll see you in a bit."

During the one-sided conversation, I turn on my side and run my fingers up and down her spine, dipping into each crevice of the bones, and gliding down the seam of her bottom then trailing back up again. I feel a sense of satisfaction when her skin breaks out in tiny pebbles from my touch.

"Stop that, I'm sore," she declares but makes no move to turn over, allowing me to appreciate the feel of her soft skin.

"You know what will help with that soreness?" I whisper into her ear as I continue to worship her body. "An orgasm."

"Keep your giant cock away from me," she protests and tries to turn over, but I use my strength to hold her in place.

Chuckling I remind her of a simple fact she seems to have forgotten. "Beautiful, I can give you an orgasm with something other than my cock. If memory serves me, my mouth and tongue did a good enough job last night. Now, lie down and relax, it seems we have all morning."

"Take the next left," Blake points out as I drive my four-wheel drive truck to her father's house.

We had gotten an earlier start than I had wanted, but after washing her languid body in the shower and her begging for me to take her against the cool tile, she had insisted we leave my bedroom.

She squirms in the seat next to me, and I know that she's uncomfortable and sore, but she craved me as much as I desired her. I didn't know how to tell her no. Every time the tingle started in my spine and my balls tightened preparing for release, I knew in a matter of minutes that I'd be ready for her again. It was a vicious cycle of pleasure, pain, and desire.

"The one with the red shutters is mine. You can park in the driveway."

The streets in her neighborhood haven't been plowed, so I'm thankful she didn't attempt to drive home last night. I don't like to think of her being stranded in the snow.

Blake hesitates as I shift the vehicle in park as if she's not sure if she should invite me inside, unsure of the protocol. Luckily for her, I make the choice for her.

"Stay there, I'll help you out."

"Okay," she whispers, the confusion in her dilemma evident.

Scooping her out of the seat, I make no move to place her in the thick snow. Instead, I hold her tightly and shut the door then carry her to the small covered entryway. Using her key, she unlocks the front door and shuffles inside gesturing for me to follow.

"I'll be right back. Just make yourself at home."

I watch her retreating back head down a narrow hallway in the small ranch-style brick home. I notice to my left is a set of images and I step closer to get a better look. Picture after picture of a growing Blake line the walls. Images of her riding a bike, wearing a leotard, performing in a spelling bee, memories of her accomplishments preserved behind shields of glass and wood.

"Who are you?" a deep voice bellows from behind me and I spin around in alarm to find a man in his mid-fifties pushing himself in a wheelchair through the opening to the kitchen. Even in his circumstance, this man exudes a sense of power that is only earned by age and a hard life.

"Hello, sir. I'm Zackary Nicholson. I just brought your daughter back before our meeting this afternoon." I hold my hand out in respect, wanting to earn a few points with Blake's father but he ignores it.

"Blake! You stayed at a man's house last night?" he roars, the pictures on the wall shaking under the weight of his words.

"Daddy," Blake says exasperatedly as she walks back down the hallway pinning an earring into her lobe. "I told you I was staying with someone I worked with." She leans down to kiss him on his cheek and his fierce demeanor instantly shrivels away to a warm smile for his daughter.

"You didn't say it was a boy."

"Dad, I'm twenty-eight. I lived away from here for six years, not including college. I'm pretty sure I can stay at a boy's house without your permission."

I can tell her father wants to argue his point, most likely ruling that as long as she's living under his roof she'll follow his rules, but a tiny redhead bounces through the front door running into me.

"Oops, sorry. Mike, you're supposed to be working your legs right now. What are you doing out of the workout room?"

"Hi, Maggie," Blake says with a bright smile, the kind I've been trying to earn from her for weeks. "This is my friend, Zack. He gave me a place to stay last night and brought me home. I hope that you didn't have any trouble making it in today."

"None at all. I'm from Alaska remember? This was easy-peasy. And nice to meet you, Zack. Blake never mentioned that she worked with such a handsome and thoughtful man."

The minuscule woman grinning before me almost causes me to blush, something I haven't done since I was in highschool and saw my first Playboy magazine.

"Don't read into it, Maggie. He works for a big box marketing firm and he's trying to get this contract for Fleming Coffee as well. Zack's the enemy.

"Anyway, I just came home to change; we have a meeting in about an hour. Then I can help put up the Christmas decorations."

I hadn't noticed at first, but now that I have a chance to look around the space I realize how barren it is. I suppose with her father's accident they haven't had the opportunity to put up a tree or decorate and it's only two weeks until Christmas. Of course, I haven't either, but my family goes all out for the holidays, so I just leave them to it.

"I can help you, if you'd like," I offer and watch as three sets of eyes turn toward me and widen.

"That's nice of you, Zack, but I'm sure that you have better things to do on a Friday night." Blake brushes away my comment as simply a nice gesture.

"Not at all and you'll probably need a truck to get a Christmas tree back here."

"Oh, we just have a fake one in the basement that we'll decorate."

Maggie and I both gasp in unison.

"You have to have a real tree," the petite therapist proclaims. "I've never had a Christmas without one."

"Come on, Blake. I'll help you pick out a great one." Blake turns her frustrated gaze to me and she knows that she isn't going to win this battle. With her father confined and unable to help, Maggie and I are all that she has.

"Fine. We can go after the meeting."

"Sounds good. We can plan to get your car this weekend; I can drive you home tonight after I stop by my office. But there is a perfect tree lot between my office and here.

"I'll see you all tonight. Thanks for the invite," I tell Blake's father who continues to eye me sternly. If I were a lesser man I would cower under his stare. I'm hoping after tonight I'm able to change his opinion of me, but I'm not betting on it.

"So, this is where the magic happens," Blake says as we step out of the elevator with a group of my coworkers. I had offered to pick her up but she insisted on seeing my office. We swerve through the field of cubicles like herded cattle until we arrive at the back corner where my area is located. I'm lucky to have one of the bigger cubicles with a view of windows on one side. On the other is my potential office that currently sits empty.

"This is me. I just need to finish up a few projects, if you don't mind. I can show you the breakroom and lounge if you want to relax for a little bit."

"I'd like to hang out here, if that's okay? I'm always interested to see how other people work. And we probably need to decide which items from the catering meeting we want to settle on."

"Sure, let's do that first," I suggest as I offer her my chair. I swoop into the empty office and grab the chair tucked under the desk and wheel it over to my area.

Blake pulls out the three suggested menus and peruses them, making notes on her likes and dislikes. But I've already settled on the menu I would like, and it has very little to do with food. The caterers brought tiny samples of each of the main dishes, and while everything was delicious, I was enraptured when Blake moaned as she licked the salmon mousse clean off her fork. I'd choose anything that would guarantee that she would be making that noise again.

"I'm really torn, there is something on each one that I believe would go over well. But I mean, do we serve fish in an aquarium? Seems a little barbaric." Though she has a point, I'm hoping that it won't dissuade her when I give my opinion.

"I vote for menu two. Everything was perfect and I think it pairs together the best."

"Really?" she asks in surprise as she spins in my chair to look over at me. Her green blouse pulls tight against her breasts straining to break free from the buttons and it takes all of my energy to tear my eyes away from her chest and focus on her words.

"Yeah."

"It was my favorite too. Well, good, we've nailed that down. I'll email the caterer and let them know. All we have left are decorations. I'll contact Lily on Monday to see where we are with the design we sent her."

The end of her pen trails along the plump rim of her lips as she focuses on something in her planner and I've never in my life wanted to be an inanimate object more.

"Okay," she says as she closes her planner and places her pen on top, instantly wrecking my fantasy. "Show me what you're working on."

Logging into my computer, I bring up the latest video campaign I'm working on and show Blake the three video advertisements that the advertising department has sent over this week. I tell her about the potential timeline and how I'm working to rebrand this company using some strategic brand placements at certain sporting events and magazines. Some of the ads I have created myself, many employees in our department splitting our duties in marketing and advertising. I know that Blake does the same in her company, only using an outside source for her video ads for filming.

Pointing to one of the ads I created last week, Blake tells me how much she likes the use of color to portray the company with a warmer feel. The business had gone through a bit of a harassment scandal earlier in the year and this was their way of bringing back the trust of their constituents.

"I like what you did here. Have you thought about doing a few testimonial ads, either on paper or video? I'd even use real customers, if possible. Word of mouth is a huge asset in their field and I think it would go a long way in restoring the customer's faith in the business. Pair those with these incredible ads you've already got flowing and I think you'll be golden. And a shoo-in for that promotion."

If only she knew that the only way I'm getting that promotion is by getting the contract for Fleming Coffee. Right now she looks so positive and hopeful, an aura surrounding her glows brightly as she works in her element. I hate to be the reason that her light dims.

"Thanks. You've reiterated something that I've been tossing around in my head for a few days. The campaign was missing something and that was it. That human piece."

Leaning closer to me, Blake's lips press against the outer rim of my ear and her breasts that I had been admiring earlier push against my arm.

"Can I tell you something?" she whispers. The feel of her breath on my ear sends a shiver down my spine and an electrical current flows down to my cock, springing it to life. "You're really hot when you're working. Like really really hot, and it's not just the suit."

I'm surprised to hear her confess something so vulnerable. I'm also surprised that she'd admit something so crass at my office. I wonder if being out of her element has weakened her, but when I turn my face toward hers, our noses only an inch apart, I find that it's the opposite. Being in my office has given her a new strength. And it is sexy as fuck.

"Stand up," I demand quietly and she quickly obeys, her chair rolling back into the desk with a clang. I slide my hand up the middle of her thigh, praying to the Lord in thanks that she opted to wear a skirt for our meeting. My fingers trail up her skin until I reach her warm and wet panties.

"Zack," she moans as I push her panties aside and slide my fingers through her slickness, hypnotized at her movements as her body rocks against my hand.

"Hearing you talk business is one of the sexiest things I've ever heard, Blake. Do you want me right now?" I ask, but I already know the answer by the way her core squeezes at my fingers when I slide them deep inside her channel. She's coating my digits in her slickness and it's causing a chain reaction straight to my erection as it hardens against my zipper, the ache almost too much. "Blake?"

"Yes?"

My fingers slip from her body and she growls at their retreat as I stand quickly, my chair shooting across the hall. My vision hazes over from desire at my need to have her. I grip her hand and stalk toward the empty office, practically throwing her inside as I shut the door and lock it. The room already smells like sex and passion, a combination of both of our wants filling the space in our unique scent.

I waste no time stalking toward her and hoisting her on top of the desk. I blindly tug her skirt up to her waist as I seal our lips together, her hot center rubbing against the large tent in my pants. Her swift fingers work at my belt and the button and zipper of my pants freeing my cock into her palm. She strokes the throbbing shaft and head, my erection jerking in her palm with each pass.

"I need to fuck you, Blake."

Her answering moan is all the response I need. I reach into my wallet and grab the foil packet I had the sense to pack this morning from the box of condoms I had stored in my bathroom as a backup. Blake leans back and removes her panties at the same time I tug my pants down to my ankles.

"It's going to be hard and fast. And you're going to have to be quiet. Can you do that, beautiful?" She nods once and I thrust my cock into her tight waiting pussy as if it's meant to be there. Her body takes every inch of me and I continue to take her at a punishing speed, but she rocks her hips simultaneously, both of us seeking our release.

I feel the tingling in my spine at the same time Blake smacks her hand against my forearm letting me know that she's close. The muscles around my cock quiver and tense in waves as she falls over the edge and I quickly follow behind her into the abyss.

I rest my sweat-soaked head onto her stomach, loving the way she strokes her fingers through my hair as I tell her, "Holy shit."

"I've never had office sex before. Something to be said for it," Blake jokes and I chuckle which has my softening cock slipping from her sex.

"Definitely something to be said for it. And hey, I just thought of something."

Sitting up with a sated smile on her face, Blake asks, "What's that?"

"You just helped me christen my new office," I jest as I remove the condom, tie it off, wrap it in a tissue, and shove it in my pocket to dispose of later.

I don't realize my mistake until I watch as Blake yanks her skirt down over her replaced panties and turns to face me, her smile long gone.

Tugging open the door to the office she says, "Yeah. I'm going to go find a drink machine. Just text me when you're ready to leave." I zip my pants and watch as she moves back to my cubicle to grab her bag.

Back at my desk, I try to work on my projects but my focus is on Blake and how I made her feel cheap and used. I had no ulterior motive when I took her into the office; I was blinded by my lust and need to have her. My thirst for her is unquenchable. Everything she does seems to turn me on, and the more time I spend with her the more rampant it becomes.

Just as I'm about to give up on my work for the day and go in search of Blake, she rounds the corner and hands me a bottle of water. I want to ask her where she's been and if she's angry, but when I look at her closely, I find something I never expected, defeat.

"Blake. . . I. . ."

"I'd like to go home now, please."

T HE RIDE TO THE CHRISTMAS TREE FARM IS quiet and tense, my irritation at Zack's comments in the office after our tryst are at the forefront of my mind. I know that I shouldn't let his words affect me the way they have, but in my moments of post-coital bliss, I had been riding a high that he quickly extinguished.

The worst part wasn't just the words that he said, I could have quickly tossed those aside. It was how those words had made me feel after experiencing something new and different with Zack. Something I had never imagined having with anyone. But he had taken that special moment and cheapened it, at the same time devaluing me.

"Here we are," Zack says, parking the car in an open spot.

I look outside the window at the red booth set up with wreaths on display for purchase and another selling hot chocolate and cookies. For a Friday afternoon, I'm surprised to find the place so busy, both booths having lines a few people deep.

"Blake, look. . . I want to apolo-," he begins, but I cut him off by opening the door and jumping down onto the snowy surface. I wish that I had brought pants to change into, but my skirt and boots will have to do.

I storm through the pathways glancing around but not really seeing any of the trees lining the route. My arms tighten closer around my body as I struggle to stay warm. You'd think with all of the fire and anger burning inside me that it would be easy to maintain the heat, but as the wind picks up and brushes light swirls of snow into the air around me, all I feel is a coldness down to my bones.

The crunching of snow behind me is the only alert I receive before Zack's hand grips my elbow stopping me in my tracks.

"Blake, please let me apologize. I didn't mean to imply anything."

"It's fine. No big deal," I reply.

"It is though. I don't treat women that way. You know that, Blake."

This man has no idea how epically terrible his apology is going. And to think I had been ready to forgive him.

"Thank you for reminding me that I'm one of many, Zack. That really makes me feel better."

"That's not what I meant and you know it. Why do you keep twisting around everything I say?"

"I'm not twisting anything."

"But you are. You're looking for a reason to stay mad at me. It's easier for you to hate me than to admit that you actually like being with me. Why is that?" he asks, stepping into my hate-fueled bubble of space, bursting through the boundary as his gloved hands land on my cheeks. "Tell me why you want to hate me, Blake."

"Because you almost destroyed my life once before and I can't let you do it to me again. There is no pain in hate, only love can cause it."

"I don't understand. What did I-,"

Interrupting Zack's question a hearty man in a heavy flannel coat walks over to us and asks if we need help finding the perfect tree. The man's long beard and twinkle in his eye remind me of every old-fashioned Santa I remember seeing on Christmas cards as a child.

"Sure," I tell him. "I have no idea what I'm looking for. Maybe seven feet tall or so. Does that sound right?" I turn to ask Zack who is staring off in the distance.

"That's the tree." He points, and the Santa Claus look-alike and I turn around to see where he is gesturing.

The three of us walk to the spot and Zack grins like a boy finding his favorite gift under the tree. Without thought, a smile grows on my lips at seeing him excited.

"This will look great in your father's living room."

Agreeing, we let the worker use a chainsaw to quickly chop down the Blue Spruce and help Zack load it into the bed of his truck.

"You didn't have to buy the tree, you know. I can afford it," I tell Zack once we're situated in the truck and heading back toward my father's house.

Zack doesn't say anything, and for a solid ten minutes, we travel without a word spoken, only the sound of the radio playing Christmas music filling the void.

"Most people will tell you that giving and receiving gifts is their favorite part of Christmas. A few may say it's spending time with family. But for me, my favorite part of Christmas was always going out to find the perfect tree. There is something about taking the time to find a tree that calls out to you, that really marks the holiday season for me.

"My dad and I would go every year out into the woods to find a tree on our neighbor's farm. We would search for hours. Well, maybe not hours, but as a kid that's what it felt like. Anyway, we'd search and search to the point I always felt like we'd never find our way home, but suddenly there it was. Like a shining beacon in the midst of these beautiful pine trees that look the same, this one tree would speak to us. It never mattered if it was too short, or too thick, my Mom would hug us and tell us year after year that we found the perfect tree.

"We'd decorate it together as a family and spend that first night watching the lights twinkle on the tree. No television, just the radio and my family. It's been our tradition since – forever. And today, I wanted to share that tradition with you."

I can feel the tears smatter along my cheeks as they rise up and over my lower lids. The emotion in his voice is raw, heartfelt, and sincere and it sends me over the edge.

"That was beautiful, Zack. I'm glad you have that with your family. They must be awfully proud of you."

His knuckles tighten along the steering wheel as he twists his hands around the grip.

"I'm lucky to have them."

"Maybe next year they can help you find a tree for your own house."

The rest of the ride ventures back into silence. It's not uncomfortable, but rather, calming. Like the soft breeze across a meadow.

We arrive at my father's home to find Maggie carrying a few boxes of what she tells us are Christmas decorations into the house. My father is shouting at her to take her crap back to her car but her laugh filters to my ears outside. I love that Maggie doesn't take anything from my father and puts him in his place.

"I have some gloves in the basement. Let me grab them and I can help you carry the tree inside."

"Blake, I've got it. Just direct me so I don't run into anything."

He hands me the stand that we purchased and as he's tugging the tree from the back I smirk as I say, "And you trust me enough to do that?"

"I'd trust you with my life, Blake." Then his face is covered by the Spruce as he lifts it into his arms.

I'm glad that he can't see the smirk wipe clean from my face because I know that I'd trust him with my life too.

Inside, we position the tree in the corner with only minimal damage to Zack's shins. He may have knocked into the coffee table after my father used his chair to push it into Zack's path. I had laughed behind my hand while Maggie smacked my father on the back of his head.

"This looks great," I tell Zack and my father spitefully nods his head in agreement. The living room is covered in pine paneling, and though I painted them white, the room still had warmth to it that only increases with the blue hue of the tree's needles.

Maggie and Zack work at untangling the lights and wrapping them around the tree while I sort through the ornaments.

It takes no time to get the tree fully decorated and as we flick off the lights in the living room, we all wait with bated breath as my father presses the remote switch to turn on the lights draped on the tree.

"Dad!" I shout as he makes us wait in the darkness before a clicking noise sounds and the room brightens in a warm glow from the tree.

"Oh, it's beautiful!" Maggie exclaims joyfully, clapping her hands in elation.

My smile is so broad that my cheeks feel the pull and ache of the muscle. I can see now how a moment like this with Zack's family would be something so special to him, witnessing the joy on his family's face when their tree has been decorated together.

I look over to find Zack's grin equally as bright as mine and Maggie's and I find him, at that instant, equally as sexy as I did when he was bared naked before me.

"Hey," I say, resting my hand on his bare forearm. Once the tree was in place, he had lost his coat, suit jacket, and tie, and had rolled up the sleeves on his pale pink shirt. Zack is definitely one of those men that can pull off wearing pink without someone questioning his masculinity. "Thank you, for this."

"I'm going to make some hot chocolate. Would anyone else like some?" asks Maggie.

"I'd love some, Maggie. Thank you," I tell her and everyone else agrees.

"Great. Would you help me, please?" she asks my father and he follows her to the kitchen with a roll of his eyes.

I feel a spark on the top of my hand and I look down to find Zack resting his hand on top of mine. I hadn't realized that I left my hand on his arm, the gesture feeling so natural, that I had forgotten to remove it.

"You're welcome, Blake. I have something I want to show you."

He reaches over to his jacket and grabs a small trinket from the pocket and then dangles it in front of me. The gold snowflake catches the light from the tree as it spins from its thread. The ornament is so delicate and fragile that I'm almost afraid to touch it.

"This is for you to put on the tree. I saw it while I was paying for the tree and I had to have it, for you."

"Thank you, it's gorgeous," I reply honestly as I take the thin piece of metal in my palm. "Help me put it on?"

Together we walk to the tree and find the perfect spot for the ornament right in the line of the fireplace so that it will catch the light and reflect it.

"Perfect." Placing the snowflake on the tree, I notice the tiny inscription that reads First Christmas, but I decide not to read anything into it.

"It looks great there. Now every time you see it, you'll remember that time you were snowed in with me." He grins devilishly.

Something about his story about searching for Christmas trees and the exchange of the ornament has made me forgive him for his words earlier; they sit in a pile of dirt covered slush just like the snow outside will soon be, melting away and soon forgotten.

Turning toward Zack I rest my hands at his stomach, fisting his shirt in my palms.

"Anything else you're hoping that I remember?"

Zack's hands find my waist and his forceful grip pulls my body closer to his.

"I'm sure there are a few other things you should remember," he reminds me before turning his devious grin into a searing kiss that should spark enough to set the tree on fire.

Just as his tongue licks at my upper lip, we break apart as Maggie cries out, "Oh!"

"Just a coworker, my ass," my father mutters as he holds four steaming mugs in his lap while Maggie pushes his chair.

Stepping away from Zack, I brush a hand down my shirt and skirt and tuck my chin toward my chest in embarrassment.

"Thank you for allowing me to help today, Mr. Holliday. I'd love to invite you, Maggie, and Blake to my family's Christmas party on Christmas Eve. My cousin, Samantha, and I are surprising my parents for their anniversary by having all of their family flown in from the west coast."

"Oh, Zack, we don't want to intrude," I point out, but he shakes his head.

"Nonsense. You wouldn't be an intrusion at all. The more, the merrier. Please say that you'll come."

I'm surprised when my father readily agrees, but I'm convinced that it's a reason to get out of the house for something other than a doctor's appointment.

"I guess we'll be there."

"Great. I'm going to head home," he tells everyone as he chugs his hot chocolate in one gulp. "I can pick you up tomorrow to get your car, Blake."

"Sure. Anytime is fine."

"Thank you all again. See you tomorrow," he directs to me as he walks out.

"Nothing going on, you say?" my father questions and Maggie and I roll our eyes.

"It's nothing, Dad. We just have to play nice until Fleming Coffee selects one of us."

"I know I've been single for a long time, sweet pea, but I know when someone is smitten, and that boy certainly is."

"No, he's not."

Is he?

"Whatever helps you sleep at night, sweet pea. Just a word of advice, don't let him have the chance to break your heart. "

My father wheels himself to his room, leaving Maggie and I alone in the living room sipping our drinks.

"Don't listen to your father. There is something to be said about having your heart broken."

"How so?"

"Because, Blake, it means that you lived."

T HOMAS SET UP A TEMPORARY OFFICE FOR Blake and me to use when we want to work together on the gala. It's both convenient and a pain in the ass. Mainly because things have been awkward between myself and Blake. And it seems as if every time I'm about to get her to speak to me about something other than the gala David sticks his nosy neck into the room and interrupts us. Which in turn puts Blake in a sour mood.

"Hey, can you look at this layout? We've received almost one hundred percent of the RSVPs, so we're going to have a full house."

I swivel my chair over to where Blake has situated herself on the far wall. I typically work using digital schemes and layouts, but on a legal-sized sheet of paper Blake has drawn out the dimensions of the main ballroom where the dining and dancing will occur. Scattered throughout the space are fifty circled tables each seating ten people. The spacing is roomy for the dinner but it doesn't leave a lot for the dancing.

"Hmm. . ." I mumble, and Blake's eyes seethe at me to question her.

"I just think. . .that maybe we could consider putting in high top tables, at least for half of the space. That would allow a larger dance floor."

"Zack," she says in an astonished tone, her eyes wide in amazement. But not the good kind. The kind that mean she's about to put me in my place.

"Yeah?"

"Have you ever worn heels? And I mean outside of your fraternity initiation." Of course, she would have known about that. The boys, David and myself included, had to walk around campus at night wearing stripper heels and bikinis.

"No, I can't say that I have," I answer truthfully.

"And did you realize that over seventy-five percent of the gala's attendees will be women?"

"No, I haven't looked at the roster."

"Well, as a woman that has worn heels on many occasions, let me enlighten you on something. A woman only wears heels to look good, not for comfort, and if you require me to stand for longer than twenty minutes at a time without the opportunity to sit down, I will end up either leaving or finding the coordinator and shoving the heel of a stiletto into his or her chest."

"So. . .tables?"

"Yes, tables."

After that decision is made, we work in silence for another half hour or so. Lily messages me about the New Year's Eve ball drop, and with the underwater theme we established at the beginning, she sends three ideas that could work for us.

"Hey, can I get your opinion on the ball drop?"

"Sure." I hear the clatter of her pencil as it falls to the desk and I imagine the sway of her hips as she sashays toward my side of the room. I gulp as she leans over my desk to peer down at my computer. I visualize her smirking at the effect she has on me, but I am too proud to look at her.

"So, we can go with any of these options." I show her the images on the screen Lily sent over and she hums as she analyzes each of them. I don't have a preference and I tell her that.

"I like this one," she points to the third image. "The bulbs along the outside look like the design of the bubble balloons."

"That makes sense. Now, what about for the explosion when the clock strikes midnight? Lily, says we can use bubbles, confetti, glitter, or mix them up."

Her bewildered gaze turns to me and I'm frozen in place.

"Zack, please tell me that amidst your revolving door of women you've at least stepped foot into a strip club."

"Well, yeah." A few years ago I tended to frequent one a lot with a co-worker when he was dating one of the dancers.

"Did you ever get a lap dance?"

I smile when I can answer this one honestly. "No, I haven't." I stifle a chuckle at the surprise on her face. "They've tried, but I usually get up and leave."

"Well, I can tell you that if we go with glitter, you and everyone else in attendance is going to find speckles of it on your body for the next umpteenth years."

"And how do you know that?"

"Every girl knows about the downside to glitter, Zack. It's not some new age technology," she barks in a tone that instantly has me on the defense.

"Okay, so no glitter. What do you suggest, Master?"She rolls her eyes at my sarcasm.

"I suggest that you message Lily and tell her we want bubbles and confetti and when you're done with that you can go find a fucking stripper and get that lap dance you desperately need."

"Oh, beautiful, you're the only woman I want grinding on my dick."

Stomping across the office, she slams herself onto her chair with a grunt. "I hope that it falls off."

"Oh, you don't mean that," I reply with a laugh.

"Zack, I'd rather have a stripper squirt a load of glitter from her vagina all over me than come face to face with your dick again."

She spins in her seat and angrily works on the rest of her part of the gala set up while I stare at her in surprise.

"So. . .no glitter then?"

A pencil shoots through the air and smacks against the wall beside my head.

"No fucking glitter, Zack. End of discussion."

"Okay then. No glitter," I mumble to myself, making a mental note to never ever mention glitter or strippers or women in general around Blake again.

As we pack up our things for the day, I spin around in my chair and ask Blake if she plans to stop by my place tonight.

"Duh."

Things changed after I handed Blake the ornament two weeks ago when I helped her and her father decorate their Christmas tree. We have been bickering like an old married couple during the day but at night, at night she gives herself to me wholly.

The snowflake had caught my eye as I handed my credit card over to the cashier as I paid for the tree. It wasn't until she placed it in my hand did I recognize the significance of the item. Snowflakes were always changing, no two were the same, and to me, Blake is as unique as a snowflake. I hadn't ever met anyone like her and I doubt I would again. She shines in the light, sparkles, glitters without any effort. But as delicate and beautiful as she is, her wrath and fury can bring a man to his knees. Which, unfortunately, I've been on the receiving end of for quite a few years.

The ornament was also subtly engraved with First Christmas – ours. Even though we aren't a couple, the meaning is significant, because she let me in to see the real her. And that was more powerful than any status.

We still have never thoroughly hashed out our differences, the reasoning we spent those first four years at each other's throats. Something I planned to remedy soon. But not tonight. Tonight I am anxiously waiting for her, her father, and Maggie to arrive at my parents' home.

Samantha had convinced my mother and father to do some last minute Christmas shopping, giving my relatives a chance to arrive without being noticed. Lily came by the moment my parents and Samantha left to help me finish setting up for the crowd.

Now we were all restless; everyone else as they waited for my parents, myself as I wait for Blake. I shouldn't be nervous to introduce her to my family, but she'll be the first woman I've ever brought to meet them.

And we aren't even dating. I'm not quite sure what we are. Every time I try to discuss it, Blake changes the subject.

Lily puts her final touches on the room, the sweet smell of cinnamon and apples aromatically flickering around the space filling it with warmth. My parents' fir tree shines brightly in the corner covered in years of handmade ornaments.

"Hey, sorry we're late. Dad was having a rough time," a soft voice speaks from behind me.

I turn on my heels to find Blake standing poised with a sweet smile for me. Her gold velvet dress hugs each of her curves and my mouth waters as I take her in.

"You look beautiful," I tell her as I lean in and press a kiss on her cheek, but I pause when I feel the bare skin of her lower back. "Turn around," I growl, and she readily obeys. The dress dips into a V, the point landing right where her spine ends. "Fuck, how am I going to be expected to keep my hands to myself?"

"Self-control?" she questions as she turns back to face me, her eyes shining bright with mirth.

"You know I have none of that where you're concerned. I'm going to have to sneak you away later."

She laughs and jabs me in the ribs with her elbow just as her father and Maggie join us. We chit-chat for a few minutes before I direct them toward the buffet table. I get them settled then Lily rushes toward me indicating that my parents will be arriving in a few minutes showing me Samantha's text.

For the first time tonight my nerves get the better of me, and I adjust my tie anxiously. Blake must take note of my nervous habit because her hand reaches out and touches my shoulder. "Hey, they're going to love this, Zack. Don't worry." Her touch and words instantly relax me, and I release the breath I've been holding.

"You're right. Thanks."

I move through the house to wait for my parents, and as I bring them to the living room and the crowd shout their surprise, all of my worries dissipate. I've never witnessed either of my parents crying, but today marks a first for such an event.

"Thank you, son," my dad acknowledges after he's had the chance to greet the family. With mom by his side, I bring them over to where Blake and Samantha stand speaking with her father and Maggie.

"Mom, Dad, I want to introduce you to Blake Holliday. She and I are working together to plan the Fleming Coffee New Year's Eve Gala."

"It's nice to meet you, Blake. That's one of our favorite events."

As they shake hands, Blake jokingly adds, "What he means to say is that we're competing for the same job and we're required to work together. We pretty much spend each day trying not to rip each other's throats out."

The small gathering laughs, including her father, and Blake instantly worms her way into my family's good graces.

I spend most of the evening moving from family member to family member though I wish I could spend my time with Blake. But every time I look over at her she's smiling or laughing, and I know that she's enjoying herself even if it's not by my side.

The night begins to wind down, and the younger cousins beg to go to bed so they can wake in the morning for gifts. Even the teens request the night to end. As most of the family leave promising to return in the morning Lily, Samantha, and I start cleaning things up.

"Hey." I hear as a pair of arms wrap around my waist. "My dad and Maggie are ready to head home. Thank you for inviting us. Your family is amazing."

Dropping the plates in my hands back on the table I twist my body toward Blake's. Her eyes are bright from the few sips of spiked eggnog she drank earlier.

"Stay with me tonight," I surprise myself by requesting.

"Zack," she sighs regretfully. "Tomorrow is Christmas. And in another week we won't be working together anymore. I'm not sure that it's the best idea."

Sliding my hand around her neck, I massage her pulse point with my thumb. "I'll bring you back before the sun rises. Just give me tonight," I beg.

"Okay," she whispers, relaxing her head against my palm.

"Hey guys, mistletoe," Samantha points out above our head giggling uncontrollably. Apparently she also partook in the spiked eggnog.

"I guess it is," I murmur and tug Blake's lips toward mine, not giving her a chance to second-guess herself.

"Merry Christmas, Zack," she says softly against my lips.

"Merry Christmas, Blake."

RENEE HARLESS

CHAPTER Seven

"**G**OOD MORNING, BEAUTIFUL." ZACK yawns as he rolls over to face me. We had fallen asleep a couple of hours ago after spending time cleaning his parents' house from the party. After he gently made love to me in the early light of Christmas Day, we had fallen asleep with me spooning him. It was an odd role reversal, but that's how we worked.

"Morning," I reply as I place kisses along his exposed chest. Something about the man's pectorals calls to me, the small smattering of hair tickling my nose. I take a deep breath and inhale his musky scent – the aroma all male, and all Zack.

"Merry Christmas."

"Same to you. I guess I should head home to spend the day with my dad."

"Stay with me just a little longer. I don't get you to myself very often."

Giggling I say, "You get me almost every night."

"Yeah, but only for a few hours before you go home. This is only the second night you've slept at my house."

"You're right. And I do like it here," I tell him as I rise up and straddle his hips.

"Do you like it here with me or my dick?"

"You, baby. Always you."

Zack and I spent a good hour giving each other the gift of orgasms this morning, and now we're both in his large kitchen as the coffee brews in the maker. I make myself at home on the bar stool where he had made his first move over a month ago as I watch him make a quick breakfast of eggs and toast.

"Are you sure I can't make you anything else? I can do bacon or sausage."

"No, eggs are good. Thank you," I tell him.

Swiping through my phone, I flick through and delete the messages from the collections agencies that have been filling my voicemail for weeks. I check my calendar for any upcoming events, and I notice that Sofie has added a new appointment tomorrow, the day after Christmas, to present our campaign proposals to the Board of Directors at Fleming Coffee.

"Hey, did you see this?" I ask Zack as he plates the eggs and brings them to the counter. I show him the screen as he takes his seat.

"Oh, yeah. I got a notification yesterday."

"Humph," I mumble around my fork as I take a bite of the fluffy scrambled eggs.

"You'll do great."

"I'm nervous. I'm afraid David is going to do something to pull the rug out from underneath me, ya know? Which reminds me, I haven't seen you and David spending much time together outside of his office hours. Why is that?"

"David and I have a strained friendship. It works when it's convenient for him. Which is fine by me because we really don't have much in common outside of the fraternity shit in college and playing baseball. When I was single, we hung out a lot at bars because it was easy, but now I don't have a reason to do those things with him. And you have nothing to worry about tomorrow. You'll knock their socks off."

"For someone who is my competition you sure seem confident in my skills."

His fork clatters as he places it on his plate and turns to face me, taking my knees and turning me toward him.

"Blake, you're incredible at what you do. You know that, and you don't need me to tell you so. Believe me, if I could convince you to work for my company I would, but I know that you wouldn't be happy there if you couldn't have your hands in every aspect of the campaign."

I know he's right. But it surprises me to have someone so confident in my abilities, and he's friends with the enemy.

"If you want to talk about your campaign I'm all ears, as a friend of course."

"Is that what you are?" I whisper.

Zack reaches out and cups my jaw in his hand and fastens his lips against mine.

"I'm whatever you want me to be."

"What if I don't like you tomorrow because you do something to piss me off?" Which very well could happen because Zack and I walk a tightrope between like and hate.

"Then I'll just carry you back to my bedroom fireman style and convince you of all the reasons why you like me again."

"What if we're in the office?"

"Then the desk will be my best friend."

"You have an answer for everything don't you?"

"Only when it concerns you. Now tell me about your campaign. You know I'm safe because I'm spending the day with my relatives and I have zero interest in going to my office on a holiday."

"Okay, but then you have to tell me about yours."

"Deal."

As we eat the rest of our breakfast I describe to Zack how I want to cast the limelight on Fleming's proactive hiring of employees that may very well be turned away by other companies. He is engaged and asks questions that I expect from the Board tomorrow, and I answer them honestly and passionately.

Zack's campaign isn't too different from many of the others used for similar companies to Fleming. His company uses the approach of "do what works," and while that will get the initial sales for the coffee chain, I don't feel that it's inventive enough for people to remember them.

Upstairs I pull on the jeans and shirt I brought with me last night in the off chance that I wanted to change to help Zack and his family clean up the mess after their party. I never anticipated staying the night. Because once I begin to hope for those nights, I run the risk of disappointment. And disappointment is only a few steps away from a broken heart.

"I can call an Uber if you want to go back to bed."

"Are you crazy? I'm not going to let some stranger take you home. There is nowhere I'd rather be than in a car with you watching the sunrise on Christmas Day," he explains as he helps me into my jacket and hands me my dress from last night in one of his garment bags.

"That sounds almost romantic."

"Well, you can't say that I never tried." Grabbing his keys from the counter, Zack opens his front door for me to exit. "Come on, let's get you home before the clock strikes midnight, Cinderella."

Laughing I swat him in the stomach as I pass and walk out into the crisp night air. In the car I spend the thirty-minute drive taking deep inhales of his manly sandalwood scent, wondering when we'll be together like this again. With the gala taking place one week from today I feel like our moments are limited, fleeting, and my chest aches at the notion.

Before I know it we're pulling up to my father's house, and Zack steers the truck into the driveway.

"Thank you for yesterday, and last night, and driving me home, and-,"

Zack interrupts me by placing his hand on my thigh, and I grow silent.

"No thanks is needed, Blake.

"See you tomorrow?"

He stares into my eyes; they say something new and unfamiliar, but I can't make out their meaning. And it frustrates me. But before I have a chance to contemplate it further, Zack grabs the back of my head and kisses me firmly, then releases me before I have an opportunity to respond.

"Yeah, see you tomorrow."

I exit the truck before Zack has a chance to get out and open my door and wave to him as I walk down the path to the front door. I turn my key in the lock and smile as his retreating headlights reflect off the glass in the windows as I close the door.

"Blake, you're here!" Maggie exclaims as she sits nestled next to my father on his chair and I stare at them in shock.

"Um. . .what's going on?"

"Blake," my father begins. "Maggie and I want to talk to you about something."

Waking up to the man of your dreams is something straight out of a fairytale. I wish that I could say that my morning with Zack was indeed a fairytale, but the moment he dropped me off at home into the romantic clusterfuck I've fallen into, I'm not quite sure what constitutes a fairytale anymore.

Maggie and my father explained that they had been fighting an attraction to each other for quite some time – been there done that. The party at Zack's parents' house last night is what solidified their feelings for each other.

Now they sit cozied up, Maggie perched on my father's lap, as I lay out on the couch watching the Christmas Day Parade. It's not that I don't approve of their new relationship, it's more that it all seems so surreal. My father has been alone for as long as I can remember, I was always his sole focus. Maybe too much of his focus, if you ask my teenage self. But now that he has Maggie to dote on, where does that leave me? But I saw the sparks between them. I knew that this change was coming and I've been prepared.

"Can we exchange gifts now?" I ask the couple who look at me in confusion. I suppose they already exchanged something in the bedroom this morning.

"I thought we weren't exchanging," Maggie says as her smile draws downward in the corners.

"It's just something small. I much prefer giving than receiving."

My family may not have much money to fall back on nowadays, but I have scraped by the past few months since my father's accident to be able to afford something nice for him. Reaching under the tree, I grab the two boxes I had wrapped the other day after Zack had helped me decorate the tree.

"Here," I say, placing the red and gold striped package in each of their hands. "Merry Christmas."

Maggie opens her gift with a flourish to reveal the dainty bracelet I found online. I ordered a few charms to dangle on the chain. A stethoscope, a medical symbol, a heart, and the Eiffel Tower – a place she's mentioned that she always wanted to see.

"This is lovely, Blake. Thank you so much. Here, Mike," Maggie holds out her wrist and the box, "please help me put it on."

"You're welcome." As she admires her gift, I turn my attention back to the fireplace. I feel a bit embarrassed about my dad's gift, unsure if he'll appreciate it or not. He'll never know that I've actually spent the past six years tucking this away for a rainy day, something for us to do together. His accident took a toll on him, but I've been bound and determined to get him on his feet so that he can fully enjoy his gift without having to use it to pay the bills.

"Blake, what's this?" my father asks, but I can't turn my attention away from the fire.

"What is it, Mike?" Maggie asks.

"A vacation package for two to Europe," my father's voice rings out astonished at the gift. "Sweetpea, I can't accept this."

"Yes, you can," I tell him flatly, turning to face the flabbergasted expressions on both of their faces. "Since I was a little girl you always talked about traveling to Europe one day and seeing everything that you can. Well, the opportunity became available. You'll spend two weeks with a guided tour seeing the best things Europe has to offer. You've given me everything that you have for the last twenty-eight years, let me do this for you.

And I think you should take Maggie with you. I can change the names on the ticket."

"Blake, no. . ." Maggie protests but my mind is made up. And I'm one of those people that once I make a decision, there is no going back. The only person that has ever changed my mind on anything has been Zack and my opinion of him.

"Yes. You'll go together and have a wonderful time. The package is good for two years; you both decide to go when you're ready. If you'll excuse me, I'm going to go catch up on some sleep."

"Alright, sweet pea. There was a package delivered for you last night, it's in your room."

"Thanks, Dad."

I practically skip my way down the hall to the small space I call a bedroom and see a shoebox-sized package on my dresser. Like a giddy teenager, I shake the box and wonder what's inside and how Zack managed to get it here without me knowing. He's a sneaky son-of-a-bitch, I'll give him that.

The thin paper gives way to my finger as I pull at the sides exposing the box beneath. Tossing the scraps into the trash by the door, I lift the lid of the box to find an envelope resting on top with the words Merry Christmas, Baby scrawled in perfect calligraphy.

Opening the flap, I remove the letter inside-a letter with printed out messages from hundreds of fraternity members all commenting on the nude picture. A few of the names I recognize and though I try my hardest not to, I read the responses. Some are favorable, saying that I could give Marilyn Monroe a run for her money with my curves and others are so hurtful I grow numb, not even realizing that I'm crying until the droplets land on the paper.

For some reason, I decide to look inside the box once more, and I'm not surprised to find a blown up version of the picture framed behind a pane of glass for all to see. I know that the gift is from David, the snake doing all he can to take me down a peg, to prove that he's better than me.

Shoving the picture and letter back inside the box I stuff it under my bed and then fall back dramatically, my need for sleep long forgotten. My stomach churns with the anxiety I experienced at David's hand. I finally took a chance and did something spontaneous, and I still feel the regret from taking the risk.

The unmistakable part that hurts the most about the surprise gift is how much of the blame rests on Zack's shoulders. David wouldn't have been able to get any of those messages without Zack's help. The only good thing that came out of the entire incident is that I saw what a cheating weasel David truly is by catching him in bed with another woman. It also gave me the determination to prove everyone wrong about the things they were saying.

So, I guess two good things came out of the scandal. But what good thing could come out of it now by rehashing the past? If anything it's just going to make me more determined to win.

A message pings on my phone and I glance over at my nightstand to check the screen.

> **Asshole #1: Hope you're having a great morning. Merry Christmas again, Beautiful. Wish you were with me.**

Turning over in my bed, I leave the message unanswered and ignore the pang in my chest as my heart shrivels in despair. As much as I hope that Zack had nothing to do with this, I know deep inside that he had to be the one to give the messages to David.

And knowing that Zack is going to crush me to protect himself and his best friend is a tough pill to swallow.

WHY DO THEY KEEP BOARDROOMS SO freaking cold? I swear I can see the mist of breath puffing from my mouth as I stand at the front of the room going over the figures I project for Fleming Coffee with this campaign. Maybe it's because the majority of the people in this room are one step into their grave and it's to keep them from rotting in their seats.

I open the floor up to questions as I finish my presentation and only one person requests a review of the cost perspectives. I've done enough of these presentations that I can do them blindfolded, and it helps that I have a general interest in assisting Fleming Coffee. Thomas has always been kind and generous to me, it helps that David is my friend, but I'd want this contract with or without him at the helm.

"If there are no further questions, I want to thank you all for your time today and I look forward to seeing you at the gala in a few days."

"Thank you, Mr. Nicholson," Thomas says as he walks over to shake my hand then steps over to his secretary and directs her out of the door. Just as I'm putting the flash drive and paperwork into my briefcase, Blake walks in.

And what an entrance she makes.

Stoic and confident she commands the room's attention as she walks through the door. I smile as she glances around the office, but her expression never falters, never shows a sign of weakness. Today's suit of armor is bold and daring, just like her. A red jacket with a matching skirt that hits just above her knees shows off her long legs coming to a stop at a pair of shoes the same color as her skin.

"Mr. Nicholson, my secretary can show you to your office unless you know the way. Ms. Holliday is going to make her presentation now."

"Sure, I'll just finish packing up. I remember the way."

"That's okay, Mr. Fleming. Mr. Nicholson can stay. He may actually learn something."

The coolness of her words alarms me and my papers scatter along the table top. After the night we spent together I'm surprised to find her so indifferent toward me.

Picking up the remnants of my presentation, I take an open seat at the table between two board members that look put out as I sit down.

"Thank you for having me. I'm here on behalf of BH Marketing, today I want to present to you your future. With my team by your side, I ensure that your company will flourish in the oncoming years. I'm sure that you've been presented with a tried and true formula that is saturating the marketing to make certain that you maintain the bottom line. But what if there is a better option? An option that will solidify your staying power with your customers? This is my plan for you.

"So, let's begin by asking yourself the most basic of business questions. What makes Fleming Coffee unique? What sets it apart from all of the other coffee chains in the area, the country, or the world?"

I'm enthralled by Blake's opening, the way she entices each person in the room to listen, to pay attention. Not just to what she's saying, but to her.

Blake begins her digital presentation focusing on the pieces she had explained to me the other day, and I take a moment to glance around the room. If I thought that I stood a chance against her, I now know how sorely mistaken I had been. These people would be idiots to go with anyone else. Even if her campaign is risky, Blake offers them something different and uniquely her own – passion. She believes in every word and emotion she speaks and portrays.

Not wanting to draw attention, I slowly turn my chair to look at the rest of the group. Thomas sits with a huge grin on his face, his pleasure at her presentation visible to any onlooker. He's in complete contrast to the snarling lips and squinted eyes of David shooting daggers at Blake. I turn my attention back to our speaker but her focus never waivers from Thomas and the board members. I wonder if she even notices the face David is giving or if she has and it's fueling her on.

She continues her presentation documenting numbers and facts of campaigns similar to the ones she's suggesting, but I'm lost in her voice. The slight huskiness is like velvet to my ears – soft, warm, seductive. Every fourth sentence her tongue peeks out between her lips to coat them, and I'm curious if it's a nervous habit, but the subtle shine left behind everytime makes her plump lips gleam. I remember how they glistened as they were wrapped around my cock Christmas night as I made love to her mouth in the moonlight of my bedroom.

Thomas claps at the end of her dialogue, same as he had for me, and I'm brought back from my internal musings about having my way with the woman standing confidently at the end of the table.

"Ms. Holliday, Mr. Nicholson, if you would please go wait in the office, the board and I will deliberate. I, for one, will say that I am thoroughly impressed by both of the presentations, and this will be a tough decision. I appreciate both of your hard work."

"Thank you, sir," Blake and I say in unison. I chuckle at the simultaneous exchange, but Blake's expression never varies.

I wait for her to pack up her things and I hold the door wide allowing her to exit the conference room. She doesn't even acknowledge my presence as she walks past. Blake walks a few feet in front of me until we get closer to the office, but once we're inside, I grab her arm and spin her around.

I was prepared to find her fired up and ready to lash out at me. What I was not prepared for is the woman in front of me with tears clinging to her lashes.

"Blake, what's going on?"

"How could you? How could you do this to me again?"

"Beautiful, what are you-,"

"No!" she shouts. "You don't get to call me that anymore."

She jerks her arm away and turns to walk over to her desk, leaving me bewildered standing in the middle of the room.

Our silence is broken as Thomas and David knock on the office door and request our presence for lunch at a restaurant in the lobby.

Spinning around, Blake assures them that she'd love to join them. All traces of her tears have vanished, and I'm not sure if I should clap or award her an Oscar for her performance.

"Can we talk?" I ask as she struts past me to follow behind Thomas.

"No."

My panic is building. Something has happened, something outside of my control, something that is about to wreck the best thing in my life, and I don't even know what it is. The worst part about this maniacal feeling is the anger that quickly follows.

I run my hand through my hair leaving it in disarray as I join the trio at the elevators. Blake stands behind the two men as they wait for a car. Leaning down to whisper in her ear, I catch her sweet scent, and it immediately causes my cock to jump.

"We will talk after lunch, come hell or high water. You will tell me what has your panties in a twist."

Murmuring her reply angrily she turns her head, our faces only a mere few inches apart.

"They can't be in a twist if I'm not wearing any."

David turns to glance over his shoulder at our exchange and narrows his eyes at our closeness.

Luckily for Blake, the elevator arrives at that moment, and Thomas ushers us inside. He and Blake stand along the back while David and I stand in the front. The ride is quiet but unsettling. The tension in the space is thick enough to choke on, and I'm thankful when we reach the bottom floor.

Thomas escorts us to the restaurant and Blake makes it a point to keep her distance from me, but even more so from David. We're sat at a circular table which leaves no place for her to escape, so I quickly take one of the seats next to her while Thomas takes the other.

"Before we order, I want to personally thank both of you for taking on this challenge. I know it is unconventional, but I do believe that it served its purpose. You see, I know that not everyone will work well together. I made the suggestion to David because if you work with my company, you may very well dislike a few of the executives who will want to offer their opinion, as well as vendors that are hard to handle. It's how you work under the pressure that gives you the cutting edge. And I am pleased to see that you both worked very well together."

"Too well," David mutters under his breath just enough for me to hear. I look over at him strangely, but he continues to peruse his menu as if he's said nothing at all.

"I'd rather not discuss business while we eat so I'll leave it up to you both to decide if you want to hear the Board's campaign feedback before or after."

"After," Blake and I both say, knowing that it will be a nightmare waiting in anticipation, but hearing anything beforehand may cause us to lose our appetite or say something that we may regret.

During the lunch, I try to reach under the tablecloth for Blake's hand, but she swats it away every time. Instead, I rest my hand on her thigh only to have her dig her nails into the top of my hand, and I screech in pain. David and Thomas look at me curiously while Blake simply takes a sip of water as if she's heard nothing.

"Sorry, bit my tongue," I lie.

The lunch is enjoyable, but I can say that I didn't taste much of it. I want to hear the Board's feedback even though I'm already certain of the answer. Luckily Blake and I still have a chance to prove ourselves with the gala happening in a few days.

"I suppose you're both ready?" Thomas asks, and Blake and I nod in agreement. "Very well. Blake, I'm pleased to say that you blew away the Board members with your idea. Unanimously they all agreed that it is unique and will set the company apart from others."

"Thank you very much, Mr. Fleming. I can't wait for you to see what we put together for the gala."

"I can't wait to see it myself. Now, Zack, the Board was equally as pleased with your campaign. The strategies you presented are foolproof, and that gives them a sense of comfort. Also, your company can be attributed to many successful expansions of businesses, that says a lot about their track record."

"I appreciate that, Mr. Fleming."

"Excuse me, I'm going to run to the restroom," Thomas explains as he nods to the waiter for the check then removes himself from the table.

"So, Blake," David drawls. "We know that Zack here has the backing of his company as leverage to help the Board make their decision. What leverage did you use to get everyone on your side? A certain picture perhaps? Maybe an updated one? I'd sure like to see it."

"Excuse me?" Blake asks at the same time I say, "What the fuck?"

"Oh, come on now. It's not a secret that you're fond of taking naked pictures of yourself. I wouldn't be surprised to hear that you're using them to your advantage."

Immediately Blake stands from the table, her chair knocking back into the table behind her.

"How dare you. Both of you," she seethes as she gathers her things. "Don't ever speak to me that way again."

I watch her move in slow motion. Blake leans forward and grabs the glass in her trembling hand. The glass lifts into the air, lights from the chandelier reflecting off the tumbler, and the water sloshes over the edge. Then, like a waterfall, Blake tosses the water inside the glass directly into David's face, wetting his suit and me in the process. I could do nothing to stop it, like a man trapped behind a cell.

Then she's gone in a flash, only the red color of her suit standing out like a speckle amongst the black and white in the lobby.

"Where did Ms. Holliday go? And why are you wet, David?" Thomas asks as he returns, flinging a linen napkin at David for him to wipe his face. "Someone explain what just happened, now."

"Your grandson said something to Blake that crossed the line and she put him in his place. That's all it is. Now if you'll excuse me, I have a woman that I need to go follow to make sure that she still plans to help put the gala on."

"Thank you, Zack."

"Don't thank me yet, Mr. Fleming."

I storm out of the restaurant and head up to the office to grab my things, wishing I had brought them down with me as Blake had. Because I'm wasting time. Wasting time where Blake and I can finally hash it out. It's long overdue.

Sitting in the driver's seat of my car I call her phone a few times, but I'm not surprised when she doesn't answer. I even try to reach out to Sofie who tells me that I can go sit on a stick and rotate. I'm not quite sure what that means, but I'm sure it's a reference to both of them being angry with me.

On a last ditch effort, I send her a message hoping that I'm able to break through to her.

> **Me: Blake, talk to me. Tell me what I did wrong.**
> **I'll come to you or meet you anywhere.**
> **Don't shut me out.**
>
> **Beautiful Girl: I don't want to talk to you.**

Me: Fine. Then can you listen?

Beautiful Girl: No. I don't want to see you or
hear from you again.

Me: You don't mean that. And we have the gala.
You have to see me then.

Beautiful Girl: I ignored you for four years, I can
do it again for one night.

Me: Blake, please. Five minutes and you can say
everything you ever wanted to me.

I watch as the little bubbles appear, then disappear, and then reappear again. A vicious cycle of hope and despair rolled into ten seconds of agony.

Beautiful Girl: You get five minutes, that's it.
Then I want you gone.

Me: Deal

And with just that sliver of optimism flourishes in my mind.

I shift my car into drive and barrel my way toward Blake's house. In my determination, I make it to her home in twenty minutes instead of the typical thirty. It isn't until I pull into her driveway that the weight of what's about to happen sits front and center.

Ten years. Ten years of wondering where I had gone wrong with Blake. We should have been friends, or at least friendly, because she was dating my best friend. But maybe that is where our problems began. Maybe their relationship was our undoing, but I can't be sure.

I know that this day has been a long time coming for me.

CHAPTER Eight

I STARE AT THE PHONE IN MY HAND AS IF IT'S going to jump out and bite me. I'm not quite sure what possessed me to allow Zack to come here and say his piece, but I'm hoping that it will give me some kind of closure. This relationship with Zack is toxic and draining, my emotions are changing at the drop of a hat, and it's too much. I can't focus on work or my family – the essential things in my life.

Stepping out into the blistering cold, I huddle into myself as I rush from my car to the mailbox, and over to the office door. I'm not surprised to find the office empty, I had told Sofie to take the week off since I was focusing on the gala.

With the mail in hand, I move through the house to the kitchen.

"Dad? Maggie?" I call out as I set the stack of envelopes on the table. When I hear nothing in response, I pull out a kitchen chair and sort through the pile. I'm not sure when the last time was that I checked the mail. I try to avoid it at all costs, afraid of what's lurking inside.

Most of it is junk, and I start a pile of ads and magazine offers while the other stack contains white envelopes with big stamps in red saying final or overdue. The one that surprises me the most is the one from the workers' compensation office. I tear through the paper, the sticky residue of the adhesive making it nearly impossible to open without ripping the envelope to shreds.

Reading through the fine print and legal jargon, it takes a moment to set in that they're finalizing their case as a non-work related injury in regard to my father. I'm not sure how they have come to the conclusion that a beam falling from an upper rafter while my father worked at his station on the assembly line isn't a work-related injury, but it seems that without hiring a prominent name attorney I'm not going to get anywhere.

The tears flood my eyes as I look at the stack of bills I have yet to open. The bills that I'm not going to be able to pay. The mortgage that is going to be defaulted on by the bank, taking our house and our livelihood.

In a moment of weakness, I curl my body over the table and rest my arms on the cold wooden surface, resting my head atop. I let the tears flow. I allow my emotions to take control and run wild.

I'm unsure of how long I've been crying, but when I hear a car pull into the driveway I grab the stack of bills and make a mad dash toward my bedroom. My dad doesn't need to deal with this right now, he's in such a happy place with Maggie. A place I never expected he would find.

The hallway is blurry through my tears, but I know the layout of this house like the back of my hand. My bedroom door slams behind me as I toss my body on the bed the same way I had thrown that glass of water at David during lunch.

That pompous asshole actually assumed that I was going to send naked pictures of myself to the Board members to win their votes. And Zack didn't say a word. Not that I gave him a chance, but that part definitely hurt. I let the pain run free until I'm all cried out.

With a bit of composure, I tear open the rest of the envelopes and sigh when I look at how far behind I am at paying these down. From what I can gather, I have a month to settle all of the utilities, with interest, make a payment on the maxed out credit card, and make three mortgage payments to bring us back on track. My bank account is already teetering on the edge of a negative balance. Everything I earn for the business goes directly into a business account, and I pay myself and Sofie from that. I've considered asking my father if he has a retirement fund we could possibly tap into, but that is a fine line I'm not ready to cross.

I glance over at my closet door where the gorgeous dress hangs that Zack purchased for me to wear to the gala. It's worth far more than I would have ever paid and I sit here considering returning it back to the store.

Standing from the bed, I walk over to the dress and run my fingers across the seams of the arms. I hate that the thought has even crossed my mind to return the gown, but right now it seems like my only option. Choking back a sob, I swipe at the tears falling unbridled down my cheeks, dripping off of my chin, and landing on the suit jacket that I have yet to remove.

In an act of fury at the situation I'm finding myself in, I unbutton the jacket and rip it from my body, pitching it across the room. As I watch the red material fly through the air, my gaze stops when it lands on Zack in my room beside my bed - standing there holding the letter from the workers' compensation office and glaring at me.

"What's all of this, Blake?" he argues as he gestures to my bed with the bills scattered on the duvet while shaking the letter in his fist.

"It's none of your concern," I huff, stomping toward my bed and gathering the bills, stacking them and then placing them on my nightstand.

"Having a roof over your head is absolutely one of my concerns."

"A misplaced one."

My cheeks are burning in my embarrassment at Zack finding out about my family's situation. That feeling increases tenfold when he says, "Let me help you with this."

"Absolutely not! I'm not some charity case."

"I never said you are. But, Blake, I can help with this. Do you know who my father is? He's one of the best attorneys in the state. I can guarantee he'd take this on."

I'm actually surprised to learn just now of his father's occupation. It's not something we've ever discussed, I always changed the subject when our conversations became too serious. Keeping Zack at an arm's length has always been the key to keep me from getting too attached. And even though he stands there devastatingly handsome and his heart is full of concern, he's part of the reason I'm here.

"I don't want your help, Zack."

"From what I gather, you don't really have much of a choice if you don't want to end up homeless."

"Stop trying to fix everything. It's not your place."

"It's my place if the woman that I care about is about to end up on the street."

"You don't care about me. I'm just part of some stupid game that you and David have been playing since college. I was just the stupid pawn that got caught up in the chess match."

Zack throws his hands in the air, exasperatedly.

"What the hell are you talking about now? I've never played games where you are concerned."

"Really?" I ask, fisting my hands on my hips, my anxiety long forgotten and replaced by fury.

"Yeah, really."

Nodding once, I walk toward him and then crouch down, sticking my hand under the bed searching for the package I received yesterday. I slap around the air until I land on the shoebox and place it on the duvet with an accusatory look at Zack.

"Recognize it?"

"Am I supposed to?"

"I received this yesterday. On Christmas. It took me by surprise, to say the least."

Confusion mars his face as he lifts the lid to the box and grabs the list of messages. For a moment I almost believe that he doesn't know what's inside. But I quickly push that feeling aside. David specifically said that Zack had stolen his phone that night and forwarded the message to the entire fraternity. And I saw Zack walk out of his room with David's phone that morning. That moment is etched into my memory for all eternity.

"What is this shit?" Zack asks. The tips of his ears are as red as my suit as his anger boils on the surface.

"What is it, Blake?" he repeats loudly, his voice vibrating in the air around us.

"You tell me." Reaching into the box, I grab the framed photo and hold it up for him to see. "Those are the messages David received after you sent my picture, the personal picture I sent to my boyfriend, to all of the fraternity. You almost got me kicked out of school. Did you know that?" I seethe. "The Dean found out and threatened to take away my scholarships. If it weren't for the fact that I had surpassed my credits needed to graduate, I would have been expelled. And it was all your fault.

"It was bad enough that you have been an asshole to me from day one, but this was too low, even for you."

I shove him hard but his muscular body barely budges, and all it does is cause me to take a step back and keep myself from tumbling over.

Zack doesn't say anything as he reaches for the picture and studies it carefully, his body trembling as he holds it in his hand.

"I . . .Blake, I. . ." he stutters, and I prepare myself to hear his excuses and ready myself to toss them away like trash. "I didn't send any pictures, Blake. I've never even seen this image before."

It's the authenticity in his voice that has me second-guessing myself, second-guessing everything. In my emotional turmoil I consider the off chance that I may have overreacted.

"What, do you mean? I saw you with David's phone that morning. And he said you had sent the picture out."

"I found his phone in the bathroom when I took a shower that morning. And David was going to say whatever he could to save his ass. Gosh, Blake, is this why you hate me so much? Because my friend lied to you about something that I never did?"

I sit down on my bed perplexed at the replay of events. Is Zack right? Did his best friend basically throw him under the bus to save his own ass? Now that I think about it, I'm not even surprised. David and I had a nasty fight following our breakup out in the quad for all of the campus to witness. And they did. I called him out on everything he had led me to believe and most of the school turned against him when all of the women he had cheated with came forward.

"You hated me so much, so it seemed like something you would do. I was so embarrassed. I sent the picture to get David's attention, not the attention of anyone else."

"I never even knew about this. I want to rip his fucking balls off."

Smirking I say, "You'll have to beat me to it."

"What did I do that made you dislike me so much?" he asks as he holds the crumpled paper in his hands and sits next to me on the bed.

"It seems stupid now but I let my emotions run wild, and the grudge stuck. For our first mentorship meeting, you showed up like fifteen or twenty minutes late. All cocky attitude and better than this mentality. I was excited to get started on our project but when you showed up late and then turned right back around to leave it flipped a switch in me."

"Wow, really? After all of these years, this is what you come back with, Blake? You hated me because I had practice, which I emailed you and the actual mentor about?"

I don't remember getting an email, but it was so long ago and I probably never saw it until after the meeting, and I was riding the high of having a date with David.

"It's the truth, Zack. I was young and obviously impressionable if that picture says anything about me. I lived under my father's reign when I was growing up. I never even had my first kiss until I got to college. But most of all I was stupid. So fucking stupid."

The pain in my chest intensifies at an alarming level; I can't even hear the clock in my room ticking away the minutes, all I can hear is the steady beat of my breaking heart. Somewhere along the way, I had forged onto a path I had never traveled, a path leading me to something greater than anything I had ever known. Love. And I had steered off that path without a way to find my way back.

Then something occurs to me; Zack egged me on as much as I did him. We were like oil and water if we were ever in a room together. Even our mentor worked to keep us separated unless there was a project we needed to work on.

"What was it about me that made you hate me so much? I still haven't figured that out yet."

Zack looks down at his hands draped between his legs, a sullen expression as if he's measuring the weight of his words.

"Didn't you know, Blake?"

"Know what?" I ask curiously.

"That you were supposed to be mine. The first time you walked into our introduction to marketing class I knew that you were someone special, someone worth holding onto. I was ecstatic to learn that you were going to be my partner for our major. I kept thinking that fate was smiling down on me. But that day by the fountain, David and I were running late for practice, but I had seen you sitting there. You were pissed, but I had never seen someone so gorgeous before in my life. I was frozen in place, afraid that you felt rejected. David must have noticed me staring at you because before I knew what was going on he had sat beside you and made you do something I had only ever fantasized about – you smiled. But it wasn't for me.

"When I walked up to the bench, you were so angry, and I knew that it was my fault. But I was mad because you agreed to go on a date with David and then, down the line, you gave yourself to him for four years. I was so angry that Fate stole you away from me and I never even had a shot. I was mean to you because at least then I got your attention, even if it wasn't the same kind you gave to David.

"He treated you like shit, and you let him. God, that pissed me off the most. He never deserved you, but I knew I never stood a chance. Even all the times I tried to tell you that he was cheating, ready to go against my word to my best friend, you had made your opinion about me, and I couldn't change it. Just like I can't now."

"I'm so confused right now. I don't know what to think about all of this."

"It's hard to forget about something that you've held onto for so many years, only to learn that the hatred was misplaced."

"I think somewhere along the way I realized that you didn't send those messages, it didn't add up. Because even after all the times that you were mean to me it was never callous, never spiteful. You did it to get a rise out of me, and then you'd drop whatever it was we were arguing over."

"I was the little boy pulling your pigtails. And I never hated you. Not the way that you think. I was just jealous. A jealous boy that didn't get the girl."

We sit in the companionable silence, neither of us making eye contact. Instead, we stare at the floor. I'm hoping that it will open up and swallow me whole. Because in my entire life I have never felt so ashamed to have been wrong all of these years.

Zack releases a deep breath that whooshes between his lips like a sigh. I don't turn my head to look at him directly but gaze at him out of my periphery. I can tell he's contemplating something as his hands run through his dark hair making it stand on ends.

"I love you, Blake. I've always loved you."

His words melt like butter over my heated skin. I turn to face him, and I'm pinned with his weary and cautious stare, no hope to be found. I take hold of his words and relish in them. It's the first time the phrase has ever been gifted to me. In the four years David and I were together, he never told me that he loved me. I'll cherish them as I lock them away in my memory. I had always imagined those words being spoken to me in the heat of passion, or underneath a canopy of stars. One of those fantasy-filled visions women have when they meet their soulmate. I never imagined it happening in a room full of lies and secrets, but Fate never seemed to be one that cared for my dreams.

Reaching out, I slide my hand against his as an offering, a chance to soak in his warmth.

"Despite everything, I know that I love you too, Zack. And, right now, I don't know what to make of it. I'm just learning that everything I've believed for at least the last six years was a lie."

"I know," he says, tugging on my hand and I lean into him, resting my head on his shoulder. His lips find the top of my hair and I melt under his kiss.

"What do we do now?" I whisper, squeezing his hand as if it's my lifeline. And after everything, I just learned, it may very well be.

"Well, first you need to think about how you feel potentially working with David if you win the contract. Which I'm sure you will."

"You don't know that. And I don't have a choice. I need this contract to help keep us afloat. I'd also never ask you to pull back. You know that I like a good challenge," I say with a smile, and it feels good. It feels different and free.

Chuckling Zack says, "I know that you do. As do I. I'm always keen on a good battle."

"Good."

Smiling at each other after everything we said should feel awkward, but it doesn't. Instead, Zack's flash of straight white teeth instantly soothes the pain and panic deep inside me, like a balm to my soul. I know that we need to work through things, but I'm amazed at how easily I can leave my hatred tucked deep in that shoebox and move forward.

He stands from my bed and tugs me up with him. His large palm cups the side of my face. I silently beg him to kiss me, to brush away everything with the feel of his lips, but the front door slams and he pulls back slightly, but not far enough away so that I lose his masculine scent as it floats around me like a curtain.

"The second thing we're going to have to do is take the letter to my father. Let me do this for you, not just because I care for you and your family, but because I love you and I know he can make this right."

I almost fight him as a knee-jerk reaction, but then I take a step back mentally. He loves me. He's doing this to help me, not to force something out of my hands. Turning my head slightly, I kiss the palm of his hand and then switch back to look into his glazed eyes.

"Okay."

"Fucking fantastic, because I'm really excited for the third thing we need to do."

"Yeah? And what's that?" I ask as I stretch out my hand to play with the tip of his tie.

"Make-up sex. It makes every fight worth it."

He yanks me forward, pressing a punishing kiss against my lips. Before I can react he's pulling back.

"Get your jacket. Time's wasting."

"Yes, sir," I tell him with a mock salute, which in turn causes him to smack my ass. I make him stand in the hall while I change my clothes quickly and grab my jacket.

All of my worries seem to fall to the wayside with Zack by my side as I place all of the letters from the workers' compensation insurance into a folder. And as I press a kiss to my father's cheek, I can't help but feel that nagging notion that the shoe on the other foot is about to drop.

But I shouldn't be worried.

Right?

MY LEG BOUNCES IN TIME TO THE SONG playing on the radio as I drive Blake to my father's office. Something about our fight seemed surreal, yet poignant. She and I were two ends of what could have been a cataclysmic disaster. But instead, we've met at a crossroads and made the decision to go down a new path. A new path where the two of us were going to work together to overcome the six years of challenges all at the hand of someone I considered a friend.

Learning that he had lied and said that I had been the one to message her photo to the fraternity cuts deep. I'm not surprised, but the pain is there regardless.

All of these years wasted and locked away because of a lie.

The pain sears deep again, my chest aching as I think that I could have almost lost her for the second time. I already know what the world feels like without Blake and it's not something that I ever want to experience again. The black and white, the muted noises, the sleepless nights – Blake brought those to life. She was the color in my world of gray and the music to my ears.

Our stomachs grumble in unison as we pass by a fast food restaurant and I look over to find her grinning widely at me.

"Want to grab a bite?"

"Yes, but something quick. I'm . . .kind of looking forward to number three on our list."

You and me both, sweetheart.

I take us through the drive-thru, and we eat along the way, just finishing up as I pull into my father's law office. He mostly deals with civil cases, but he dabbles in corporate law every now and then. This isn't the first time he's taken on a workers' comp case like this, nor will it be the last.

Escorting Blake inside, I ask the receptionist to buzz my father and tell her that it's important. Blake grips my hand tightly as the woman sneers at her. The receptionist is young, probably right out of college.

"Previous member of your harem?" Blake whispers in my ear.

"She wishes," I joke in return and Blake playfully slaps my shoulder in response.

"What a surprise!" my father exclaims as he steps in the lobby. "It's good to see you both." He embraces Blake and then me before guiding us back to his office where Blake and I take a seat.

"Now, what is this important news? Are you getting married?" he asks, and Blake chokes on her own saliva.

"No, Dad. Actually, it's important because Blake and her family are about to lose everything. Her father's accident is being denied by the company's workers' compensation. He can no longer work due to the injury. I am hoping that you can go through these and get it all sorted."

"I'd be happy to."

Blake hands over the file with all of the medical bills and the documentation from the company explaining the accident.

"I can't pay you, sir."

My father can be ruthless in the courtroom, always standing up for those that he believes are innocent, but he's also one of the most caring and kindhearted men that I know.

"I would never ask you to," he tells her with a smile crinkling the edges of his eyes.

I can tell that Blake is getting choked up, so when she grabs a tissue and excuses herself, I let her go willingly.

"I'll be able to get this turned around tomorrow. She'll get her money next week if I have anything to say about it. Won't even need to go to court, they just need to be reminded that we're not here to play around."

"Thanks, Dad."

He drops the folder on his desk, steeples his fingers, and then looks at me carefully. It's the same look he used to give me growing up when he knew I had done something wrong but I wouldn't fess up to it.

"You love her?" he asks.

"I do."

Nodding, he turns in his seat and reaches into his briefcase before pulling out a small velvet bag.

"If you love her don't let her slip through your fingers. You may not get a second chance."

"Or third," I want to tell him, but I keep my thoughts to myself.

"This belonged to your grandmother. She wanted you to have it."

I make to reach for the bag, and as my father places it into my waiting hand, he covers it with his own.

"I like her. Not just because she's beautiful and smart, but because she compliments you in every way. I can see how happy she makes you and, in turn, that makes me happy."

The door to the office creaks open, and Blake steps inside as I grip the bag and clumsily try to stuff it into my pocket without dropping it.

She looks at me curiously, and I'm confident I look like a deer stuck in headlights at almost being caught.

"Sorry about that," she apologizes to my father.

"No problem. I looked over everything quickly; this is pretty cut and dry. I'm going to send them a certified letter to resolve this issue quickly, or they will see me in court. I'm sure you will have your payout next week to cover the medical expenses, and your father's company's disability should kick in shortly after."

"Really?" Her chin quivers at the realization that everything is going to turn out alright. She has fought an uphill battle, and now she's going to be rewarded for her persistence. "Oh my gosh, thank you so much."

She jumps from her chair and prances around the desk to hug my father, who embraces her warmly while shooting a wink in my direction.

Pulling back, he holds a tearful Blake at arm's length. "Blake, I wish you had come to me sooner. Don't ever hesitate to ask for help when you need it."

"Yes, sir."

"Now, you two get out of here. I'll see you at the gala next week. Your mother and I can't wait. Which reminds me, give her a call later, Zack."

"Yes, sir."

I usher a beaming Blake out of my father's office, and just as we step out of the doors, she spins around and jumps into my arms.

"I don't think I'll ever be able to thank you for what you've just done," she says, peppering kisses on my face. I carry her over to my car and press her against the side.

"I can think of a few ways," I add just as I take her mouth with mine.

Blake and I stumble into my house as we work to paw each other's clothes off. She barely gave me a chance to press the stop button on my car to kill the ignition. At least I think I shut it off, but with Blake's hands sliding under my shirt to feel my chest it seems almost inconsequential. I am trying to hold myself together as her fingers trail around my abdomen, but as she leans forward and nips then sucks at the sensitive skin on my neck, I'm a goner.

I'm not sure if it's the years of loathing swept away or that we've professed our love for each other, but either way, we can't make it to the bedroom fast enough. I work her out of her coat as she walks backward with my guidance to my bedroom and she rips apart my shirt, the tiny buttons pinging off the hardwood floors, and tosses it away. Her shoes follow, as do mine, quickly trailed by my belt. We're like Hansel and Gretel leaving a trail of breadcrumbs, except we're leaving clothes without any intention of finding our way back to my kitchen any time soon.

Reaching out, I pop the button of her jeans and secure the zipper between my fingers, tugging down. I pull away as she shimmies her hips, the denim cascading down her legs into a pile at her feet.

"Holy fuck. That was one of the sexiest things I've ever seen."

She's a vision standing before me in a pair of nude lace panties barely peeking out from underneath her cream-colored silk camisole that she had worn under her suit today. The ends of her luscious brown hair fall around her waist, some of the smaller strands curling around her breasts, beckoning my gaze to drop to the nipples trying to poke through the barrier of her lace bra.

My control is at an all-time low, as she sucks her lower lip into her mouth, biting on the pink flesh, and it snaps like a rubber band. I launch myself at her, pressing her body against the wall and punishing her mouth with a searing kiss. She's always had a flavor so sweet it's like pure sugar, but right now she tastes like the most heavenly of desserts.

Blake rocks her hips against my growing erection, and I reach down, trailing my fingers across her thigh before I lift it upward, nestling it against my waist. I thrust my body against her heated sex a few times, and I'm thanked by a husky moan that vibrates all the way down to my aching cock.

"Touch me, beautiful," I beg of her, and my girl slips her hand between us and strokes the outside of my pants before unbuttoning them and slipping her hand past the material. A hiss escapes my mouth as her small fingers brush against my throbbing head.

"Fuck," I drawl as she strokes me up and down, twisting her palm everytime she reaches the head and then trails back down to repeat it again.

Her caresses pick up in speed as I remove my undershirt, baring my chest to her glazed over eyes.

"You're so fucking sexy," she tells me, and my cock jumps in her hand at the compliment.

"I could say the same about you."

Her grip on my shaft never waivers, and I have to force myself to take a step back, or I risk coming all over her hand and my pants.

"Take this off," I direct, picking up the ends of her camisole. She follows dutifully, and in one swift movement, I'm mesmerized as the cream silk is pulled above her head and her hair falls in waves back down onto her body. Her breasts heave with each breath she takes as they push against the confines of her bra. She looks like a fucking angel, but I know she keeps those black wings tucked away when she wants to play.

Silently I reach out and slide my hand between her legs, luxuriating in the dampness of her panties as they soak through from her essence. I do this to her. I have her soaking in her own heat, her sex craving me. I slip a finger past the cotton barrier and her body jerks as I glide it across her folds.

"You're so wet for me," I begin. I skim the tip of my finger into her channel, and her restraint disintegrates. Blake sandwiches my head between her two hands and she fastens our mouths together. Teeth clash and tongues swirl as we fight for control. My finger swirls around her clit as she rocks her hips against my cock hanging freely from my pants. I know that if I don't have her soon, I'm going to drive myself mad.

Removing my hand from her sex, I grip the edge of her panties in my fist and tear the lace apart. Blake doesn't even shutter, she reaches down and pushes my pants and boxers past my hips so that they sit on my thighs. Wrapping my arm around her waist, I lift her body into the air as I guide my cock toward her channel. She's so wet that my erection glides effortlessly inside her. I give her a moment to adjust, but only that, because my body is shaking as it restrains its need to break loose.

"Tell me you want me to fuck you right now, Blake. I can't hold back much longer."

Instead of words, Blake answers me with a bite to my shoulder as the tips of her fingers scrape across my back. I moan at the pain, and my cock grows even further.

Situating my hands on her thighs I lift Blake's body an inch or two, my cock almost to the point where it slips free, but then I thrust back inside. Her channel quivers with each plunge as I pound her against the wall, the momentum shaking the pictures hanging by their nails in the hall. She feels so good, too good, my body can't hold back its need to release.

"Oh my gosh, I'm coming, Zack," Blake cries out, her nails digging into my shoulder at her powerful push over the edge. I let the tingling in my spine take over, and I follow her over the crest a moment later.

Blake rests her limp body against the wall, my hold on her the only thing keeping her steady. Without removing myself from her body, I carry her to my bedroom where I manage to lay us on the duvet together. I finally allow myself to slip free from her sex and I lie on my side facing her.

"We didn't use any protection," I say softly, trailing my fingers across her chest.

Her solemn face rolls over to gaze at me. "I know."

"Are you okay with that?"

"I'm assuming that you're clean? I'm not on anything, but I should be fine."

"Yeah," I whisper, moving my fingers to trail up and down from her breastbone to her navel. I won't deny the clench in my stomach when she said that she should be fine. For a split-second, I imagined her with my child growing inside.

One day.

"Okay," she replies as we lock eyes and my hand moves over to her waist and rest on the soft dip in her figure.

"I'm going to marry you one day, Blake Holliday."

I expect her to be surprised, shocked even, but I didn't foresee the small smile to grow on her mouth or the twinkle in her eyes to shine like the North Star my mother always points out in the night sky.

"What makes you say that?" she whispers.

"Because I've loved you for ten years. There is no one else I'd rather love for the rest of my life."

I don't give her a chance to respond, maybe I'm too nervous to hear her answer, instead I seal our lips together and show her with my body how much I love her.

T ODAY IS OUR LAST DAY IN THE FLEMING
Headquarters office before the gala. I am going
through the event checklist before I head over to
the venue for a final walkthrough with the planner and
Lily for the design. We are lucky that Lily closed the
aquarium early so that the event team we were able to
hire can start tonight.

I'm packing up the few files and papers I had
stacked on my desk as I feel a pair of arms wrap around
my waist.

Nipping then licking the pinched spot on my
neck, I close my eyes and rest my head back onto a set of
strong muscled shoulders. Zack asks, "When did you get
here?"

We spent the last weekend in his bed, only
leaving his room when we ordered takeout. But on

Monday reality set in and we both went our separate ways for work. The last time we spoke was yesterday evening when I told him to thank his father for the check I received in the mail. A check covering all of my father's medical bills, the utilities, and interest.

We still messaged back and forth, our bickering now a form of foreplay, because by the end of the day we're so hot for each other I barely make it through his door before he's stripped me of my clothes and buried himself deep inside me.

"About an hour ago," I reply. "I wanted to go through a few things."

"I don't like you here by yourself with David lurking around."

"I came straight into the office. He doesn't even know that I'm here."

I'm not sure if Zack has confronted David about the present and the lies, but he assured me that he would take care of it.

"I know. I just left his office."

I pull away from him, my skin instantly missing the feel of his lips against my neck.

"What were you doing in his office?"

"Just catching up."

"How can you even want to be in the same room as him? If he walks by me, I want to gouge his eyes out. I figured with the way he lied about you that you'd feel the same," I seethe.

"I do, but my job hangs in the air, and I'm not going to do anything that ruins my chances at getting the contract. It's the same reason you're here making sure that the gala is perfect for tomorrow night."

Damn, he's right. Keep your enemies closer and all that jazz.

"I'm sorry. I'm overreacting."

"At least you're sexy when you do it."

"You think I'm sexy all the time," I tell him, reaching out to rest my hands on his hips.

"I only speak the truth. Now, let's finish packing up your things and make our way over to the venue. I know you're dying to do a walkthrough. And then, my beautiful girl, we have plans."

Shoving my folders into my bag, I ask, "What kind of plans? Does it involve me, you, and your bed?"

"Eventually. But I am taking you on a proper date. We kind of did things backward."

He helps me into my coat and his rough fingers stroke along my jawline.

"I hate to disappoint you, but I don't put out on a first date."

"Well, then it's a good thing we don't follow the rules."

The aquarium is empty when we step inside. Utterly vacant except for a few stacked tables ready to be moved into the banquet room. Not a single person in sight. I grip Zack's hand tightly, squeezing his fingers as we continue to step into the darkened space, the only light coming from the fishtanks lining the wall.

"I feel like we're in a Stephen King movie. If I see two little girls standing in the hallway, I'm making a run for it. Everyman for himself," I tell Zack who chuckles as if I've said a joke. It wasn't a joke. I don't jest about twin ghosts. Or any ghosts for that matter.

There will be a red carpet for the event at the entrance, we were lucky enough to have a few local and national news and entertainment channels interested in the event and the charity that the company will donate toward at the end of the night. It will also help Fleming Coffee get their name in the press. The carpet will follow down the hall leading the guests to the main hall for the event.

We follow the path we've mapped out and find the banquet room. Lily stands in the center with the event planner discussing something to do with the ceiling. Zack and I walk over and greet them. The event planner eyes

Zack hungrily but he pays her no mind, far more interested in the digital layout on Lily's tablet that she holds in her hand.

"What do you think about this, Blake? Because of the electronic system, we may need to move the stage over about two feet."

I look over his shoulder and nod, agreeing that the change will work and not interrupt the rest of the setup. Lily takes us around the rest of the space and setups, assuring us that they have everything under control. We meet back up with the planner in the banquet room after an hour has passed.

"Do you all need anything else? I can see that the tables and stages are starting to get set up. When do you think you'll have the decorations ready? I'd like to come by in the morning."

The event planner says that her team plans to work tonight and tomorrow morning and that we can come by anytime. I don't miss the wink she shoots Zack; subtlety is not her best asset.

"Well, thank you both. We will see you tomorrow."

"Do you want to drop your car off at my house or did you just want to follow me to the restaurant?"

"What would you like me to do?"

"Live with me, but that would be too soon. We haven't even been on a date," he jokes. "Let's drop it off at my house."

It only takes about ten minutes to get to Zack's house, but his property seems so far removed from the city. If I didn't know any better, I'd think we had traveled hundreds of miles away. I lost his car along the way, but I find his house easy enough.

I suck in a breath when I see him resting against the side of his car with his arms crossed against his chest. He looks so masculine and intense. My headlights cast him in a warm glow as I pull up beside his car and park.

"You're beautiful, you know," I tell him as he swings open my door and offers his hand to help me exit the vehicle. "You were standing there looking like you belong in the secret service."

"Is that so?" he snickers as he opens the passenger door to his car.

"Yep. It was hot."

"I'm going to take that as a compliment."

"As you should."

The car starts in motion, and I'm anticipating heading back toward the city, so I'm surprised when Zack takes a turn in the opposite direction out of his neighborhood.

"Where are we going?"

"A surprise," he teases with a smile. It's one of my favorite smiles, right behind the sexy smirk, and the one he gives to himself when he thinks no one is watching.

About twenty minutes later we pull up in front of a house with about ten other cars lining the driveway.

"Where are we? Is this someone's home?"

Exasperated by my nosiness, Zack utters my name, "Blake."

"Sorry."

We exit the car and walk hand in hand to the covered porch. Just as we step onto the wooden planks the front door opens and a host ushers us inside with a smile. He helps us from our jackets and then directs us to the stand where Zack gives him his name.

"Yes, Nicholson. Right this way."

For a restaurant out in the middle of nowhere, I'm surprised to find the space filled to the brim. I'm pretty confident that I even notice the mayor and her husband sitting at a table in the corner.

As I take my seat my head twists and turns as I take in the space wanting to absorb all the nuances that I notice.

With a laugh, Zack says, "Go ahead and ask."

"Oh my gosh," I say in a hushed voice. "What is this place? And is that the mayor?"

"This is Bountiful Roots. It's a local farm to table restaurant that I had the pleasure of working with over the summer. The owners won a televised cooking show and used their earnings to open up this place. Not only does the restaurant help the community but it's an entire experience. And yes, I'm fairly positive that is the mayor, she's a big fan."

"Wow. How did I not know about this place?"

"You were gone for a long time," Zack answers.

"So how does it work?" I ask, just as our server steps up to the table and goes through the menu options we can select from. I go for walnut and honey drizzled Halibut and Zack opts for the grass-fed Angus beef.

We make small talk until our meals arrive, going over details for tomorrow. Zack and I take our first bites simultaneously, and I moan in delight when the sweet fish hits my tongue.

"That's my favorite noise."

"I may break my first date rule after this meal. It's remarkable."

"Maybe that was my ploy all along," Zack taunts, and I shake my head while taking another hearty bite of my dinner.

"So, tell me. What was it like living on your own in Atlanta?"

"Hmm. . .freeing. That's the best word I can use to describe it. Leaving after. . .everything. . .allowed me to start fresh. No one knew me. No one had expectations, you know? I got to do things I had never tried. I got to experience things that you can't here in Charlottesville."

"If you had the chance would you go back? If there was nothing here to tie you down."

I ponder his question for a moment because my first instinct is to say, "Of course," but now that I'm back I can see all of the things that make our town unique. Not just the city, but the area my father raised me in. The community. So, that's what I tell him.

"Do you think you would have left if you knew it was David all along? Or if the picture situation never happened?"

"So many questions," I reply, relaxing back into my chair.

"You don't have to answer."

"I'm just teasing. But here's the thing, I've never thought about it. It happened, and I moved on. I never let it hold me back from anything. What about you? Would you change anything? Maybe to move out of the city for your internship? Explore the world?"

"I wouldn't change anything about my life."

"Really?" I ask, shocked. Most people have at least one or two things they wish that they could change.

"I didn't say I don't regret anything, but I wouldn't change them. Every moment has made me who I am, taught me invaluable lessons."

"That's a good point."

"And, Blake, if I changed anything in my life then I may never have had the chance to have you."

"Damn, you're so getting lucky tonight."

He smiles that devilish grin that I love and flags the waiter down for the check. No dessert for us tonight, we have better things waiting for us at home.

Of course, once we arrive back at Zack's home, he makes quick work of removing our clothing and feasting on my sex as if he's a man starved, not one that just spent two hours eating dinner at an award-winning restaurant. After I come on his tongue he flips me onto my stomach, hoists my hips into the air, and plunges his cock so deep inside me I swear I can feel him in my chest.

He's like an animal - wild, unbridled, feral - taking what he wants and giving me what I need. It never takes him long to bring me to my release, his cock rubbing against that sensitive spot along my inner walls. This time he comes right after me and collapses his body on top of mine, the sweat from his body dripping onto my back.

"Best first date ever," I joke, and Zack joins me in laughter.

Lifting up off my body, he kisses my shoulder and then lies down beside me, wrapping his arm around my waist and tugging me toward him, my back to his chest.

"Last first date ever."

THE MOONLIGHT SHINES OFF THE CURVE OF
her hip where the sheet had fallen free from her
body. Just watching the small movement of her
lips pucker with each breath sends a flicker of excitement
down to my cock. But today is a big day for her, for us.
The gala is something that we've planned together for the
last two months, and all our hard work will come to
fruition tonight. My mind is racing with last minute
thoughts and ideas, the curse of having a late night
creative mind.

I slip free from the bed and check to make sure
that I don't wake Blake. She moves slightly, but only to
turn onto her stomach, exposing her bare backside to me.
God, I love her ass. I'm hoping that she'll let me take her
there one day. The caveman in me wants to claim it as
mine.

Leaving the bedroom, I tiptoe out of the space and
slowly shut the door then make my way down the hall,
grabbing my pants along the way. Flicking on the light to
the living room, I'm surprised to find many of the
pictures hanging lopsided on the wall, and even a lamp

knocked over. She and I had apparently been a little overzealous in our need to have each other last night.

In the corner of the living room sits a desk I had set up with my laptop and a stack of files resting on top. Usually I'm one to finish my projects with time to spare, but recently my heart's just not into it. The company and I have chalked it up to the stress of trying to nail the Fleming Coffee contract, but I wonder if it's something else. My mind seems to be otherwise occupied by a beautiful brown-haired woman softly snoring in my bed.

With my pants still in hand, I take a seat at my desk and reach into the pocket feeling the supple velvet bag beneath my fingers. Grabbing the string, I tug the bag free and place it on the desk, staring at it as if it's going to do something miraculous. My curiosity gets the better of me, and I open the bag, dumping out the navy blue velvet box inside.

My father asked me to not look at it, but that's like handing a kid an ice cream cone and telling him that he can't lick it. That's a battle anyone is going to lose.

Taking a deep breath and closing my eyes, I flip back the lid of the box, smiling as the old hinges squeak with the movement, then I open my eyes one at a time. I'm not sure why I'm worried, my grandmother has remarkable taste, as did her mother before her. Focusing on the ring before me, I pull it free from its confines and bring it closer for a better look.

The yellow gold has antiqued, giving it a softer hue. The marquise cut diamond is surrounded by ruby baguettes. I'd say the diamond is at least four carats because it's about as big as my fingernail. The ring is perfect for Blake. I can see her wearing it with the class and grace that it deserves.

Inserting the ring back into its box and baggie I reach for a key that I keep tucked under my desk with a magnet and unlock the secret safe stashed behind the side drawer. Once the ring is safely inside, I open a few of the files and try to get some work done.

"Hey, what are you doing up?" a sleep filled voice asks from behind me.

I set my ad design aside and turn in my chair to find Blake leaning against the corner of the hall leading to the living room wrapped in the sheet.

"Hey, beautiful," I call out with my hand poised in the air for her to take, beckoning her closer. She walks over and grasps my hand like it's second nature and I tug her onto my lap, nuzzling my face into her sex-mussed hair.

"What are you working on?" she asks, picking up the design I had been playing with.

"Just a few campaigns that have deadlines approaching. I haven't been feeling very creative recently."

"Yeah?"

She lifts my folders and scans the marketing campaigns inside, flicking from one folder to the other shaking her head in disbelief.

"These are crap."

I laugh into her hair because I definitely agree. I tell her how they were passed down by another director, and I was tasked with providing some of the ad designs, but he created the full campaign.

"It is the main reason I want the promotion, I'd get to create everything from scratch and follow it all the way through."

"They're wasting your talent because advertising copy like this is not it. You have great ideas, Zack, and you're being pigeonholed into the same crap everyone else is doing. Don't you want to do something unique and different?"

Sarcastically I ask, "Wow, maybe I should start my own company?"

"Shut up. I just think you have more potential than what they're seeing. Because this," she says holding up one of the folders, "is not it."

"I agree."

"Why don't you come back to bed? We have a busy day ahead of us."

She removes herself from her perch on my lap and grabs my hand, pulling me behind her as she walks back to the bedroom. Flicking the light switch to the living room as I pass, I blanket the house in darkness. Once she crosses the threshold of the bedroom, I purposefully step on the edge of the sheet, yanking it free from her body. She screeches my name as I expose her naked body and I can't help but reach out and brush my fingers over the peak of her breast. She takes a shuddering breath at my touch, and I know that we won't be falling back to sleep anytime soon.

Reaching across the bed the sheets feels cool to the touch, and I pry open my eyes, squinting when the blinding sunlight pours through the window.

"Morning," I hear from the doorway, and I turn over in bed to find Blake leaning against the jam with nothing but one of my T-shirts on. I cement the vision to memory because it's one of the sexiest things I have ever seen.

My voice is scratchy as I say, "Good morning," as if I have gone days without a sip of water.

"I was going to make us breakfast, but I wasn't quite sure what you like to eat."

"I'll eat just about anything."

I watch as the blush pools on her cheeks probably remembering how I feasted on her pussy last night.

"Pancakes?"

"Sounds good." Sitting up in the bed I wave her over to me. "Come here."

Once she's in arm's reach I yank her toward my body and bring our lips together. When my tongue peeks out seeking entrance to her mouth, I'm surprised when she pushes me away.

"Sorry, we have a busy day ahead, and if we go any further, we'll never leave this room."

Damn, I hate when she's right.

"Fine. I'll join you in a sec."

Blake sways her hips as she exits the room, giggling as I groan from my spot on the bed.

"Devil woman!" I shout at her, and I can hear her melodic laugh all the way to the kitchen.

A few minutes later I've tugged on a pair of sweatpants, and I join her in the kitchen as she plates a few pancakes.

"Smells delicious," I tell her, leaning my hip against the island.

Turning around with a full plate poised in the air, she eyes me up and down, her jaw dropping during the perusal.

"Are you eye molesting me?" I joke and reach out to take the plate from her hands.

"Absolutely. By the way, you should always walk around like this. No shirt and gray sweatpants is one of the hottest things I've ever seen. I should take a picture and post it on social media."

"I'd rather that you didn't. Now, come join me for breakfast."

After our meal Blake begins to pack up her things so that she can run home then meet me at the aquarium to help set up for the gala. I hate watching her toss her items in the small duffle bag. I like having her stuff in my space. Even the seven bottles of shampoo she placed in the shower, or the different scented lotions on the bathroom counter, don't bother me. Because she comes to my bed at night and tucks herself against me, where she should always be.

On a whim I reach into the junk drawer I keep in the kitchen as a catchall and fish out a small item I know is tucked in the corner.

"Blake."

"Yeah?" she replies as she zips up her jacket to fight off the cold outside.

"Would you. . .I mean, I'd like it if. . .dammit," I mumble, unable to find the right way to ask her.

"Zack? What is it?"

Taking a deep breath, I squeeze the metal key in my hand and ask, "Would you move in with me? Please?"

"Really?" she questions and I notice the sparkle of excitement growing in her eyes.

"I like having you here, and I want you here all of the time."

"I like being here too. I'd love to move in. I just need to sort things with my dad."

"Of course," I tell her as I place the key in her palm. She grips it as tightly as I had been holding it.

"Wow, I can't believe we're going to live together." She sighs dreamily, her eyes shining brightly.

"I love you, Blake."

"I love you, too. I should get going. I'll meet you there in about an hour."

"Okay, beautiful."

I'm a little late when I walk into the aquarium to help set up, I needed to take care of a few things before I left the house. One of those items was to make sure that I don't tackle Blake and find a secret place for both of us. My hunger for her is insatiable, and it seems to grow more ferocious the more times we come together.

The roll of carpet is propped along the main entrance's wall ready to be rolled out tonight. The banner for photographs hangs from its stand in front of the guest services desk, masking the wooden eyesore shaped like a shark.

Peeking in the room that is going to be used for the silent auction, I'm pleased to see it's set up complete. Across the hall is the banquet room and I'm surprised by how far everything has come. The stage is set up just off the center of the room, and the parquet dance floor is in place. Someone is standing on a ladder setting up lights just off the edge of the stage where the band will be playing.

Samantha was able to talk one of her customer's bands into performing tonight. Blake and I were thrilled to know that there will be live music.

The custom ball drop we ordered is being brought in on a dolly from behind me, and I move to the side to let them pass, noticing that Blake trails behind them.

"Wow."

"I know, right?" I ask her as I wrap my arm around her waist affectionately, but she quickly steps to the side, my arm dropped back down. I look at her in question, but she just shakes her head and mouths "work." I nod my head in understanding even though it hurts that I can't hold her close.

"This turned out way better than we had planned."

"I definitely agree. I just got here and was going to see if Lily or Caroline need any help." I'm actually surprised that I don't see Caroline, the event planner, around barking orders. I worked with her on the last event, and that was one of the reasons I wanted to use her again. She gets things done.

Blake and I walk toward the kitchen area where the caterers are beginning to set up their dishes and hundreds of bottles of champagne sit boxed on the counter. But there's no sign of Lily and Caroline.

Together we walk back out toward the main entrance, and I slip my phone from my pocket ready to dial Lily when six huge bags of helium-filled balloons try to fit through the door. Blake and I rush to hold the double doors open and allow them to file through.

"Hey, I was wondering when you guys were going to stop by," Lily says as she peeks from behind the balloons.

I reach over and take them from her hands and Blake does the same for Caroline. The others carrying their masses file down the hallway to the room.

"What can we help you with? From what we can see it looks like everything but the linens and balloons are ready to go."

Caroline pulls out her phone and scrolls through what I am assuming is her checklist.

"Actually, those two items and then double checking with the caterer that all of the food and diningware are accounted for, that should be it. You did a great job coordinating everything, Mr. Nicholson."

"Well, it was a team effort. Let us carry these balloons back for you, and we can start stringing them together."

With the group effort, we are able to get the air bubble centerpieces secured to the coral and kelp displays that will sit in the center of the tables. Caroline ushers Blake and I from the space, guaranteeing that we will be thrilled with the finished product. It's hard to see it come to life with the room still in disarray, but I know she'll do great with the job, so we willingly leave.

"Are you ready for tonight?" I ask Blake as we walk to our vehicles.

"Yeah. I never went to prom so dressing up and dancing tonight will sort of be my chance to relive it."

"You never went to prom?" I ask her astonished. Hell, it's a rite of passage for most teens.

"No. No one asked me, and I was too shy to go alone." She shrugs.

"Well, I'm glad that I get to be the one to take you tonight."

"Me too." Blake stands on the tips of her feet and presses a gentle kiss to my lips before she turns to open her car door and slip inside.

"I'll see you at six, beautiful."

As she nods, I close her door and make my way to the driver's side of my own vehicle with my phone pressed to my ear.

"Dad?" I begin when the call is answered. "I don't care what strings you have to pull, but I need to find a limousine for tonight."

RENEE HARLESS

CONTORTING MY BODY IN AN UNNATURAL way, I finish yanking the zipper up the back of my dress. I breathe a sigh of relief when it reaches the end.

The deep purple dress fits perfectly, just as the store associate claimed it would. The long sleeves finish at points on the top of my hands and only go halfway up my upper arms, leaving my shoulders bare. The bodice is fitted tightly to my body like a second skin and the material crisscrosses over itself at my midsection then flows into a soft sinuous skirt with a slit up the thigh that shows a glimpse of my leg when I walk.

At first, I had planned to wear a pair of black shoes, but then I remembered the pair of champagne colored heels tucked in the back of my closet that would be a perfect match for my clutch.

Glancing in the oversized mirror I keep propped in the corner, I swish my body back and forth feeling like Julia Roberts from Pretty Woman. Leaning closer to my reflection I inspect my makeup again. I'm not one to wear a lot unless the occasion calls for it, but I've been practicing by watching a few videos online, and I think I nailed my smokey eye for the night. I painted my lips a burgundy color to compliment my dress and left my hair down, curling the ends the way that Zack likes.

Stepping out of my room, I run into Maggie in the hall, who draws her hand to her mouth as the looks me over.

"Oh my. You look stunning, Blake. Go to the living room, I want to take pictures."

I haven't spoken to my father yet about moving out, but I'm hoping that with our finances now taken care of that he'll ask Maggie to move in. I've noticed changes in him since they came clean about their relationship. He seems more open, carefree, loving. It's a change that I hope sticks around.

"Sofie?" I ask, noticing her in her full-length princess gown standing in the middle of the living room. "I didn't know that you were stopping by. You look beautiful."

As an employee of my company, Thomas offered to let Sofie attend the gala. She also plans to make a large contribution to the silent auction after I mentioned that there is a spa getaway up for grabs.

"Alright, girls. Get together," my dad suggests just as Maggie holds her phone above his head. Sofie and I smile until our cheeks hurt waiting for Maggie to finish.

"Beautiful," my father whispers and if I didn't know better, I swear that I can see him swipe at his eyes as he turns his chair around.

"Well, my ride is waiting out front, but I wanted to come to see you before you get pulled in a hundred different directions tonight. You look like a movie star."

I wave goodbye from the door as Sofie covers herself with a fur wrap and flounces to the towncar waiting on the street. Back inside I take a seat in the living room on our old worn out sofa, my elegant attire clashing with the brown plaid design. My father and Maggie laugh loudly at something in the kitchen as they eat their dinner and I stare down at my phone. My old insecurities come back to haunt me as I glance at the clock seeing that Zack is fifteen minutes late.

He wouldn't stand me up, would he?

Another five minutes pass and I start to get worried. I frown when I unlock my screen and I don't find any missed messages or calls from Zack.

Just as I'm about to bring up my date's number, a knock sounds on the door and I clumsily toss my phone in my hand like it's a hot potato then it tumbles to the floor and under the couch.

"Shit," I say as I fall down to my knees and stick my hand under the furniture to retrieve the phone, my evening gown covered behind sticking up in the air.

"Well, that's quite the sight," Maggie giggles as she moves to open the door.

Feeling the electronic in my grasp, I stand up quickly and readjust my gown and hair hoping that I haven't ruined anything. Just as I'm flicking a piece of dust from my sleeve, I hear Zack gasp in surprise.

"Holy shit."

"Hi," I reply bashfully as I take him in wearing his custom tuxedo.

I love Zack in a suit, but in a black tuxedo with a bow tie, I'm practically foaming at the mouth.

"You look stunning, Blake. I. . . I'm speechless. I've never seen anyone more beautiful," he tells me as he approaches, his gaze moving up and down my body and then repeating the motion.

He reaches out to twist the end of one of my curls as I say, "The dress is lovely."

"You're lovely, the dress is just material." Leaning toward me he kisses my cheek and smiles. "I'm sorry that

I'm late. I planned a surprise that took a little longer than it should have."

"Surprise?" I question just before Maggie comes back into the living room with her phone poised in the air.

"Can I get a picture, you two?"

"Of course, I'm recreating Blake's missed prom." He wraps his arm tightly around me, and I rest my hand on his chest looking at the camera, then I take a chance to sneak a glimpse of him, tilting my head up only to find him looking down at me with love and affection pouring from his eyes.

"Alright, you two, have fun tonight."

"Thanks, Maggie."

Zack helps me into a long coat that Maggie let me borrow; I never had the need for one. He escorts me outside, and I stop dead in my tracks when I see what's waiting on the street.

"Is that a limo?"

"That's my surprise. You said you missed your prom and tonight we're reliving it. And you can't go to prom and not have a limo."

"You did this for me?" I ask teary eyed, hoping that my makeup stays in place as the moisture pools on my lower lids.

"I'd do anything for you. Sorry that I was late, I had to work some magic to find a driver tonight."

"This is one of the nicest things anyone has ever done for me."

"I love you, beautiful. Now, let's go party."

He grabs my hand and helps me to the car. "Hey, Zack. I love you too."

A wheezing noise echoes in the cavernous space as Zack presses the button to raise the privacy screen between the driver and us.

"Now," he starts as his hand creeps up the skirt of my dress settling on the heated area between my legs, "I hope that you brought extra lipstick because I absolutely plan on fucking you in this car."

A look of surprise catches on his face as I lift my leg over his body and straddle his hips.

"I always come prepared."

Thirty minutes later the car pulls up in front of the aquarium and my nerves begin to quake. Tonight's gala holds all the cards and not just the reaction of the guests is at stake – but my chance for this job that I desperately want. I'll be happy and supportive if Zack lands the gig, but ultimately it will still hurt because my business is counting on this contract to turn things around. I can't get by on the small campaigns that we've been given. We need something bigger and of notoriety and Fleming Coffee will do that.

"How do I look?" I ask Zack. I had to reapply my lipstick twice. The first time was because we went at it like two horny teenagers in the back of a limo on prom night – how ironic. I'm pretty sure that there is a burgundy ring around his cock. The second time was while I was reapplying the first time. Zack said watching me run the tube of lipstick over my lips drove him mad.

"You look thoroughly ravaged."

"I better not!" I shout in horror as I pull out the small compact mirror in my clutch, but Zack rests his hand on top of mine halting my movements.

"I'm just teasing. You look perfect."

The door to the car opens, and Zack steps out first then holds his hand out for me to take.

"Zack, remember. This is a work event."

His eyes narrow and I know that I've hurt his feelings, but I don't want to risk our being a couple to keep me from the job. "I remember. I can at least escort you inside."

"Did I tell you how sexy I think you look in that tux?" I tell him while we walk up the steps.

"Hmm. . .wait until you see it on the floor later."

We both laugh and the tension from moments ago fades away.

Once we step inside the building, Zack hands our coats to the coat check and retrieves our tags, then we're assaulted by the press as we begin our descent down the red carpet. Many simply want pictures, and a few ask who my dress was designed by. Once I reach the end, I turn around and find one of the entertainment reporters leaning closely into Zack, whispering something in his ear that makes him laugh. My chest pinches at their interaction, and I feel chilled as if someone opened a window to the winter sky.

Unable to watch any longer, I turn and take a stroll through the auction room where many of the items are already past their reserve bid. Zack had a great idea to invite some executives from companies in the area and surrounding cities. His plan seems to have paid off for the charity.

I exit the auction room just as Zack finishes his promenade down the carpet.

"Hey, there you are."

"Sorry, you seemed a bit occupied." I gesture toward the reporter who continues to eye Zack even though she's speaking with the Governor.

"Wait a second; you're the one that told me to keep my distance because this is a work event. Make up your mind, Blake." If we were at any other place, I would probably growl at him and say something that I regret. Instead, I turn around and try to enter the banquet room.

"I know. I just think-," I begin as I step past the entrance and all of the air whooshes from my lungs. "Oh wow."

"Wow is right."

Zack and I stand together taking in our masterpiece. The ceiling is draped in light blue and white linens mimicking the soft waves of water. The balloons look as if they're drifting toward the sky, their tethers completely invisible to the naked eye. White spotlights shine up the columns with rotating white lights circling around the room. It's as if we've been transported to an underwater experience.

But the pièce de résistance is how the entire right wall is open to the shark exhibit. When Zack had Lily show us this space months ago, I was floored with the breathtaking view. Even tonight it seems just as magical if not more so.

"I'm pretty certain Caroline knocked this out of the park."

"She did," I agree. "But it was our vision and design that she brought to life. Come on, let's find some seats and grab some food. I'm starving."

I'M NOT SURE WHAT I EXPECTED WHEN WE arrived at the gala, but this wasn't it. I knew that Caroline was talented, but she has masterfully created the vision Blake and I handed her only a couple of months ago. She took our tiny, hand-scribbled, piece of paper with our concept and turned this banquet room into an underwater spectacle.

Blake and I wave and shake a few hands when we're recognized by a few of the partygoers as we walk toward a table in the corner that looks empty. She quickly sets down her purse, which she tells me is the universal sign that the seats are occupied, and we load some plates with food.

We talk through dinner, mostly gossiping about some of the attendees, but it's lighthearted and leaves us both laughing. From our seat, I spy a few pieces of the chocolate cake both Blake and I agreed was sinful when we tasted it a few weeks back, and I move quickly to snag two pieces.

The dessert is just as delicious as we both remember and when Blake takes her last bite, I reach up to wipe away a piece of chocolate that has gathered at the corner of her lips. For a split second, she smiles and leans her cheek into my palm.

"Well, doesn't this look cozy," David claims as he stands beside our table, resting his hands on the back of one of the chairs. I worry that he's going to do something to embarrass Blake, but we're saved when Thomas walks up to stand beside his grandson.

"This is a wonderful party. You both did an amazing job, don't you think, David?"

He snarls his reply, "Yes, splendid."

"I hope that you both decided to take the night off and enjoy yourself. Tonight is about fun and bringing in the New Year."

"You're right, sir. We were just enjoying a piece of the chocolate cake. I highly recommend it."

"I will have to grab a piece for me and the misses. Now, come with me, David. There are a few people I would like you to meet. You both enjoy yourselves."

When David and his grandfather turn around Blake and I both lean back in our chairs and take a deep breath. And under the curtain of the tablecloth, I reach out beside me and grab her hand, smiling when she clasps it willingly.

Sofie joins our table with her date, an Olympic Snowboarder, and occupies the majority of the conversation. I'm not even sure most of the time what's she's talking about but Blake and Jaydon, her date, seem to be enthralled – or very good actors. But I'll sit here listening to Sofie drone on as long as Blake leaves her hand tightly in my grasp. Neither of us has moved from our positions in almost an hour.

Leaning toward me Blake whispers, "I need to use the restroom."

As she stands, I feel the sudden loss of her hand like losing my own limb.

I begin to follow, but Blake shakes her head and tells me to stay.

I watch her retreating back as she weaves her way through the crowd and then disappears. I wait for what I believe is a solid minute and stand from my chair.

"Wow, forty-five seconds. I'm surprised you lasted that long," Sofie jokes, and I just shrug my shoulders.

The bathroom is down a hall located next to the auction room. I follow the path until I find the women's restroom sign and I stand against the wall waiting for Blake to exit. An older woman startles when she walks out and sees me standing outside the door, but then she smiles hungrily as her gaze travels up and down my body.

"If only I were younger," she murmurs as she walks past and drifts her hand across my abdomen.

I've never been accosted by a woman older than my grandmother, but there is a first time for everything.

I'm still in shock from the forwardness of the woman that I almost miss when Blake walks out of the door.

"Well, this is a-," she begins, but I cut her off as I grip her arm and yank her down the hall. As we maneuver through the maze of corridors I look back briefly to find Blake laughing with a brilliant smile on her face. I've never seen her look so carefree and gorgeous, it's something that I mentally promise myself to make happen repeatedly.

"Where are we going?" she asks as we turn another corner.

"I don't know," I tell her, but I do. I'm searching for Lily's office because I know that it's on the other side of the aquarium and the door locks. We had met there once to go over the contract. Finally, I spot Lily's door at the end of the hall, and I pick up our pace, practically running to the wooden structure.

I flip the door open and shove our bodies into the darkness before slamming the door shut behind us. I don't need light to find Blake in the room, my instincts easily locate her in the obscurity of the room, and I grip her waist, pulling her against me. My lips seek out her neck, needing to taste the sweet skin where it meets her shoulder. With the way her dress exposes her skin, it's been taunting me all night.

"Zack," she moans. "We don't have a lot of time."

"I know beautiful. I just need to taste you."

Dropping down to my knees, I shove the skirt of her dress to her waist and raise her leg onto my shoulder. My nose skims against the outside of her panties, inhaling her sweet heat and loving the way she shivers in my arms.

"Oh God, Zack," she moans, her hand delving into my hair, grabbing the strands tightly in her fist sending a current straight to my throbbing cock.

"I need to taste you."

I don't wait for her response. Instead, I grip her panties and rip them from her body.

"You owe me two."

I'm barely listening to her, my focus solely on the scent drifting from her sex, the slick feel of my fingers as they slide through her folds.

My mouth latches onto her clit as I thrust my fingers in and out of her sex. I work quickly, bringing her over the edge before she has a chance to realize that she's approaching her crest.

"Oh my gosh, Zack, that was. . ."

I stand and wipe my mouth on the back of my hand. "It was amazing, incredible, feel free to insert any remarkable explanation that you desire."

We laugh as I reach out to search for the light switch, flipping it and bathing the room in illumination. Blake adjusts her dress and runs a hand through the strands of her hair.

"We should probably get back out there."

"Yeah, before David starts to look for me," I tell her, knowing my friend will want to have a few drinks, but as I take a glance at my watch, I notice we wasted a lot more time than I thought. I must have lost myself in her pussy and misplaced time.

Silently we leave Lily's office and maneuver our way back to the banquet hall where the music is pulsing louder than before. Couples dance to the lively beat.

I drop Blake's hand as we pass through the opening to the room but I step closer to her and press my hand to her lower back. With luck on my side the song changes to a slower beat, and I look down at the gorgeous angel by my side and lead her to the dance floor.

"Dance with me," I demand as I tug her into my arms and tuck our joined hands against my chest. We sway to the music, and I imagine how it will be when we're dancing our first dance as a married couple or when we stand in a nursery rocking our baby to sleep. The images are as clear as day, as if I'm standing in the middle of them.

The singer announces that the ball will drop in one minute and we will celebrate the New Year. The crowd gathers on the dance floor. Hundreds of people stand shoulder to shoulder in the center of the room watching a projection screen of the ball drop in Times Square in New York City. Our own ball creeping down its pedestal ready to light up at the strike of the New Year.

But my mind isn't on the new year or the crowd or the celebration about to take place. It's solely focused on the woman gazing up at me with hope and love in her eyes that I know mimic the look in mine.

"Five. Four. Three. . ."

"I love you, Blake. Happy New Year."

"I love you too, Zack.

An explosion of confetti and bubbles float around us as the crowd goes wild and the year changes. I know that by this time the servers are passing around more glasses of champagne for the celebration, but there is only one thing on my mind.

"Let's go home."

Smiling up at me Blake replies, "Yes."

T ODAY IS THE BIG DAY. THE DAY THAT CAN
change the course of my business and my life.
Zack and I haven't spoken much about what
happens after today's meeting, after one of us is chosen to
lead this campaign for the next ten years.

Fleming Coffee has kept us on our toes up until
this point, but I have a really good feeling about this
meeting. Not just because I believe that my ideas are
better than Zack's and his company's, but because I also
received glowing references from the few companies that
I have worked with.

Zack and I didn't spend the night together, both
of us agreeing that we needed to tackle some outside
work before going into the meeting downtown at ten this
morning. But we decided that this upcoming weekend I
would begin moving my things into his house. It was

strange not sharing his bed last night, something we had become far too familiar with.

Sifting through my closet, I pull out my plum colored skirt with a matching jacket and a cream-colored silk camisole. Purple has always been my lucky color. Grabbing my black stilettos, I carry them from my room and down to my office.

Just like I do most mornings, I greet my father but he doesn't need me to help him with breakfast or to get ready, he now has Maggie for that. I feel a twinge of sadness knowing that my father doesn't require my assistance the way he once had. Things are changing, moving forward, and I hope that today is a move in the right direction for me.

As I step into my office space, tossing my shoes beside my desk, I pull up my computer and get to work corresponding with some of my clients. My email dings with a note from a local consignment shop that has opened a few new locations in the surrounding area. The owner thanks me for the idea of using a pay per bag and coupon deal for the holidays. It worked just as I had intended, to get people into the shops. I smile under her warm praise and silently pat my back at a job well done.

"Good morning." Sofie breezes into the office.

"Hey."

"Are you ready for today?"

"I am."

"Good, because they would be idiots not to hire you. You're amazing at what you do."

Smirking at my friend I say, "You have to say that because I sign your paycheck."

"No, I don't have to say it because you're my best friend and I'm not the kind of person to tell you something just to make you feel good."

"Yeah, I know. I do have a good feeling about today though. Oh, and Kathy with the consignment shop sent us a message saying that our campaign worked fabulously."

"As we knew that it would."

On my desk, my cell phone dings with an incoming message and I see Zack's name flash across the screen. I finally changed his name in my phone from Asshole to Zack when he persisted enough, he also may have held off on giving me an orgasm until I agreed to change it.

> **Zack: Good luck today. I can't wait to fuck you after we celebrate.**

> **Me: What if you get the job?**

> **Zack: Then we are still celebrating because I'll get a promotion.**

Me: Maybe I won't want to celebrate then.

Zack: Yes, you will. You love my cock – and me.

He's right, I do. On both counts.

Me: Good luck to you too.

Zack: Thanks, Beautiful.

"That must be lover boy."

"How do you know that?" I ask Sofie curiously.

"You get this goofy grin on your face whenever you talk or think about him."

I'm about to argue with her until I catch a glimpse of myself in my computer screen and realize that I have a smile stretched across my lips, my cheeks bright and rosy. If I had a white beard, I'd be Santa Claus.

Knowing that I'm not going to argue with her, Sofie nods once in triumph before she takes her seat and begins to work.

"Actually, we probably need to figure out what is going to happen once I move in with Zack." She drops her pen on her planner and looks at me inquisitively. "I mean, I'm okay continuing to work here in the garage, it's just quite a distance from Zack's, and I know that you live halfway between both."

'Would he let you work out of the house? Maybe convert one of the spaces?"

"I don't know. I could look at renting a space too."

"You could. You know I'll go wherever you go."

"I just feel bad about dad."

"Why?" his voice booms at the office entrance. That man has a sixth sense for when he's being talked about.

I tell him how Sofie and I were discussing possibly moving the office and how I feel bad because he put so much effort into converting the garage.

"Don't worry about it, sweetheart. I'm sure Maggie and I can come up with something to use it for. I've always wanted a man cave. . ."

"I really do appreciate everything you've done for me, Dad."

"I know you do. And not a day goes by that I'm not thankful of all the ways you have taken care of me."

Moving over to his chair I lean down and hug him tightly, surprised at how firmly he returns my embrace. My father has never been overly affectionate, a hug and kiss growing up only when it was necessary. But his accident has changed him, made him more appreciative of his life and loved ones.

"I'm sure you'll get it all figured out."

Piping in, Sofie asks, "Now the real question is. . .are you prepared for your meeting?"

My eyes light in surprise when I take a look at my watch and realize the time.

Scrambling around the room, I grab my briefcase and the file for the Fleming Coffee Campaigns, shoving them inside before snagging my purse and car keys.

"Wish me luck."

My dad mumbles but Sofie laughs lightly.

"Hey, Blake," she calls out. "Shoes." Sofie points at them when I turn to face her. Looking down at my bare feet I realize that I'm so preoccupied that I almost left barefoot.

Smiling I slip my feet into the black pumps and wave goodbye. "Thanks."

I greet the receptionist on the main level with a wave; it's the same woman that had been there the first time I had come on the property. She smiles at me when I flash my temporary badge and head toward the elevators.

The car stops on the second floor, and I'm surprised to see Thomas walk inside holding two cups of coffee.

"Good morning, Mr. Fleming."

"It's a pleasure to see you, Blake. I went to grab a cup of coffee for myself and David. I'm looking forward to today. David is meeting with Zack as we speak."

"Oh," I say surprised. "I wasn't aware that we were meeting separately."

The doors open for the sixth floor and Thomas gestures for me to exit ahead of him.

"He wanted to go over a few things with Zack prior to the meeting. But truthfully, I think they're just shooting the shit in there," he chuckles. "I left David with the hard decision, I gave my input, as did the Board, but as you learned at the initial meeting, this is David's project." Great. "But I don't think you have anything to worry about," he says with a wink.

I hadn't realized that Zack and David maintained their friendship. Zack doesn't speak of him often, if ever when we're together. Normally, knowledge like this would bother me, but Thomas puts me at ease.

We stop in front of the conference room, and Thomas walks in ahead of me, handing his grandson his coffee.

"Well, I will leave you to it. It's been a pleasure working with both of you these past few weeks, and we're honored to have either of you working with us."

"Thank you, sir," I tell him, Zack responding the same way, and then Thomas turns to leave the room.

"So, I have a proposition," David begins, and my skin crawls at the way his eyes skim across my chest as if he's imagining something far different than the contract we're meeting about.

David leans down, stretching his custom suit across his back, and pulls out two stacks of paper from his briefcase. I scan the top of the document and shock simmers then quickly gives way to rage.

"What is this?" I pose as I point to the top of the contract that reads Contract for Creative.

Zack looks up from his contract with his sexy grin on his face, one of my favorites, but I'm fueled with too much fire to admire it.

"That, Ms. Holliday, is the contract I have decided upon. The Board, for some reason, are set on your campaign. They find it new and refreshing."

"Then I should be the one with the job offer, not Zack," I shout, standing from my position at the table.

"Sit down, Blake," Zack says calmly, and I pin him with my gaze.

"Excuse me?"

"Yes, Blake," David continues, "sit down." When I make no motion to take my seat David murmurs, "Fine, have it your way. Zack and I discussed the possibility of his team recreating the campaign, and they are on board. We have generously offered to pay you five thousand dollars for the creative ideas behind your campaign."

"What?" I screech as the proposition finally sinks in.

Piping in, Zack adds, "You would be listed as a partner, Blake. It's not a bad idea, and I've seen this done before."

"I'm sorry, was this your game all along, Zack? Did David tell you to seduce me and get me in your bed so that I'd be more willing to sign on the dotted line?"

"Blake, that's not what-," He begins standing from his chair and moving from the table coming around to my side.

"I can't believe I trusted you and your fucking lies. God, I thought we had worked past everything, but no, it's still all the same shit it used to be. Were you even telling the truth that you had no idea about the photo?" He reaches me and holds out his hand to touch my arm, but I roll away from him. "You know what? Fuck you both. I don't agree to anything, and if I see even a glimpse of my idea, I'm going to sue your asses."

I storm from the conference room to the noise of Zack shouting my name and David calling him back in.

"I have ways to convince her to sign. Don't worry," David's voice echoes and I can imagine his slimy sneer as he says it.

"I don't give a fuck about that," Zack replies as I finally make it to the elevators and wait for the doors to open. Damn things are never here when you want them to be.

"Blake! Blake, wait. Let me explain."

Spinning on my heels, I face the lying man that stole my heart just as he approaches. Fueled by my wrath, I bend my leg and swing my stiletto covered foot right toward his family jewels. Swiftly he catches my foot before I'm about to inflict, most likely, permanent damage and releases it to fall back on the ground.

"Blake," he repeats, not expecting the left jab that I land on his nose, the crunching noise beneath my fist quite satisfactory to my ears.

"You can explain it all to your coworkers when you have to tell them why you have a busted nose and black eyes. But I don't want to ever hear from you again."

He stands there holding his nose, blood pooling between his fingers and dripping onto the white marble floor. My heart lurches in my chest because he's still breathtakingly gorgeous.

"You don't mean that."

Luckily the elevator doors open and I step inside, the situation suddenly sinking in and sitting heavy in my gut.

Zack tries to stop the elevator as David and Thomas join the crowd forming in the lobby around us; a crowd I hadn't realized had appeared. The tears begin to trickle down my cheeks even though I try to push them away and remain stoic.

"I hate you," I tell him and the lie burns in my mouth. "I don't want to see you ever again."

Zack stands before me in shock and hurt, his own eyes watery as my words sink in.

As the doors begin to close, I see David approach and toss an arm over Zack's shoulder. I turn away and face the side of the car.

"Don't worry, she's just another woman, there will be plenty of those."

The surprise at David's cruelty causes me to turn my attention back to them only to find Zack taking a swing at David and colliding his fist into David's chin.

"Screw you," is the last thing I hear before the doors close and the elevator descends to the entrance.

Exiting the car, I realize that I've left everything in the conference room. I walk over to the reception desk, and the receptionist sends me a sympathetic glance as she calls up to retrieve the items for me. Not wanting to run into Zack, I decide to hide in the women's restroom for ten minutes.

And the great thing about an empty restroom is that no one is in there to see my heart shatter.

"WHAT WAS THAT FOR?" DAVID shouts in the lobby of Fleming Coffee in front of his employees and executives, including his grandfather, the CEO of the company.

"This is not what we discussed."

"So what? I went with what was best for our company."

"No, you did what was best for you. Just like you always have and I'm done with it."

"What's going on here?" Thomas asks, the usually carefree man turning into the stern and forbidding CEO at the drop of a hat.

"Your grandson tried to manipulate Blake and me. We had spoken this morning about my company running the campaign but under Blake's tutelage. It's not unheard of since my company has so much clout in the industry."

David groans some more about his chin and how he's been assaulted, but no one in the crowd pays him any mind. No one except his grandfather who sneers toward him and tells him to stop his caterwauling.

"Continue, Zack. I'm very interested in what my grandson deems as common business practice." Thomas crosses his arms and stares down at me, and for the first time, the man I've known for so many years actually makes me feel anxious.

"So I arrive with a particular idea of what was going to happen today at the meeting and when Blake walked in I was actually excited for the chance to share with her that we would be able to continue working together. But when David handed us our contracts, she noticed that her contract was terminating her rights to her creative piece and ideas. That she would have no part of the campaign except for a small mention if the moment ever arose.

"What you witnessed was her storming off because she was made to feel cheap and as if she had been stolen from. And your grandson made her believe that this was part of my idea and had been playing her into it the entire time.

"And now she's gone and out of my life. You're lucky I don't murder your grandson right here."

Thomas nods through my entire speech and when I'm finished, I feel wrecked. Like a shell of myself because I know, without a doubt, that getting a chance to fix this mess with Blake is practically impossible. She's been hurt enough by the both of us and trusting me again isn't something that she is likely to do.

"This true, David?"

The man I once considered my best friend shrugs his response which only infuriates his grandfather more. The older man storms toward David and grips him by the ear, a move I've never seen in person, only in movies, and drags his grandson back toward his office.

"Zack!" Thomas shouts. "Wait in the conference room for us."

"Yes, sir," I say as I make my way toward the room, surprised to find Blake's jacket, purse, and briefcase resting in their same place from where she had set them down at her arrival. I consider taking them to her house after with the hopes that she'll speak to me and let me explain everything. Except just as that thought crosses my mind a security guard in the building strolls in and collects her things.

"Hey, are you taking these down to her? Is she still here?" Jumping from my seat, I bombard the over-muscled security guard with questions. He looks me up and down then proceeds to leave the room without a word.

Slumping into my seat, I can't comprehend how everything turned to shit in the course of a few minutes. Blake and I had come so far, and most of our past was left where it belongs – in the past. Until David threw every ounce of the insecurities that Blake and I had in a blender without a lid, so it spewed out into the room, coating everything in its mess.

Strolling into the room with a natural air of confidence, Thomas takes a seat across from me. "Sorry,

Zack, I had some business changes that needed to happen ASAP."

"I'm sorry about that."

"About what, son?" he asks.

"About hitting David. I shouldn't have acted out in that manner. That wasn't professional, and I do apologize."

"No need. He deserved it."

Thomas surprises me, and I know he can tell it on my face because his answering chuckle relaxes me.

"I would like you to reconsider our offer. I think you could do good work for what we are planning. It's obvious I was partial to Blake, but I'm not disappointed in the decision."

I take a good look at the man before me. A man that I admire and respect, and I won't lie to myself, it hurts to know that I am not his first choice.

"What if I turn it down?"

"Then you leave me the tough decision of starting from scratch without my second in command because he has since been demoted without the option of ever taking over. I am very saddened by this turn of events. Not just for the business but for my family."

"How long do I have to let you know my decision?" I ask, weighing my options.

"I'd prefer sooner rather than later. Ideally, end of the week."

"Okay, I will let you know."

Two weeks. Two weeks of utter and complete agony as I resituate my life - my life, my career, my world. It's been an undertaking. I'm one of the lucky few that has a Trust left by my great-grandfather. A Trust worth millions of dollars that I have never wanted to touch, and still have no need to touch now with my significant savings, but it's there just in case. Which made my decision to turn down Fleming Coffee an easy one.

I was doing it for all of the wrong reasons. Sure, the competition in the marketing world is a thrilling chase, but there is more that I want to do with my schooling. More that I am passionate about. I have been researching what it would take to open my own business, one that focuses on event planning, but will still come up with marketing game plans and advertising on smaller scales for companies. A few of my clients have agreed to come on board if and when I start my own business.

My father had agreed to go over some of the licensing requirements to begin the process, but first I need to finish clearing out my car with all of my belongings from my cubicle. When I gave my two-weeks notice, the same day I told my boss that I had no plans to cheat someone out of a contract that clearly should have gone to her.

As I packed my things into boxes my last day, I had stood in the office that should have been mine and remembered taking Blake against the desk. If I knew that I could have gotten away with it, I would have stolen that desk and brought it home as a memento of all of the great things that I lost.

Just as I set down the last box and flip open the flaps to the top my doorbell sounds. I move to open the door, and I'm surprised to find Sofie standing on my porch with a malicious expression.

"God, you look like shit too."

"Excuse me?" I ask.

Except she's right, without Blake by my side at night, I haven't slept for days, and it's showing. The light smattering of facial hair has turned into a full-blown beard at this point.

"You and Blake both look like shit."

"How is she?" I ask her.

"I'm not here to discuss that she hasn't been the same since you two broke up. I'm here to tell you that she wants to see you. Here." Sofie holds out her hand with a key and note resting together. "Don't be stupid. You love her, and she loves you. You both messed up."

"Why didn't she come?"

"Because she's stubborn just like you and is afraid you won't hear her out."

I miss her, but I probably wouldn't have listened to her.

"Read the note. I'll be seeing you."

I watch Sofie get into the back of a towncar and pull away then I flip the note in my hand. It's nothing more than an address scrawled in her delicate handwriting.

I toss the note and key on my desk and go back to emptying the boxes from my office. I get about halfway through before the taunting of the key and note get the better of me and I grab them from the desk and head toward my truck. If this is where I have to go to get closure, then so be it.

The drive is on the outskirts of the city, about halfway to Blake's father's house. I double check the paper and my GPS when I pull up to the nondescript building and make sure that this is the place I'm supposed to be.

Parking across the street from the building, I walk to the entrance and twist the key into the lock, opening it up to a large, under construction workspace.

Just as I'm about to go in search of Blake I hear the voice I've dreamt of for the last two weeks.

"Zack?" she asks, stepping from the hallway. "You came." The relief in her voice is evident and the crack in my heart splinters even farther.

"I was. . .curious," I say, holding up her handwritten note.

"Come with me," she says excitedly, holding out her hand for me to take. I stare at it for a moment but give into my desire to touch her. It's been too long since I've felt her and her palm fits against mine as if they were made to match.

We walk down the hallway until she stops at an office at the end. The door is cracked, and she steps back allowing me to walk through. Her name sits on a nameplate on the desk and behind the wooden structure is an engraved piece of driftwood with her company's logo scrawled across.

"Wow, this is great," I tell her, not entirely sure why I'm here.

"Zack," she begins and pops herself up onto the top of her desk. "I wanted to apologize to you so many times. I realized once I got home and saw the key to your place on my dresser that I had made a colossal mistake, but I didn't know how to go about it. Nothing that I came up with was good enough, big enough, to apologize for not trusting you.

"So, I thought, maybe I needed to get my life in order to prove to you how sorry that I am. I started sending out resumes, completely ready to close my business. But then I got a call from Mr. Fleming, with the contract offer.

"All I could think was, 'What would Zack do?' I turned him down but then he said something that had me thinking. He said that you turned him down. You said that you couldn't do it without me. Is that true?"

"Yes, it is."

"Good. Then I have a-,"

"Blake. Why am I here?"

Her eyes glaze over as she glances down at her jean-clad knees before she jumps down to stand in front of me.

"Zack, I'm sorry. I'm sorry for not listening to you. I'm sorry for not trusting you. I'm sorry for not loving you the way that I should have. I'm an idiot, and I want the chance to make things right between us."

Instinctively I reach up and tuck a chunk of her hair behind her ear.

"It's okay to be vulnerable every once in a while, Blake. It doesn't make you any less strong or any less of the person you want everyone to see. But with me, with me, I want the gentle and delicate side I've grown to love."

"Do you. . .do you still love me?"

"I never stopped, beautiful. I was worried that you'd never give me a chance to tell you that."

"How come you didn't call or message me?"

"Truthfully? I wasn't sure that you'd answer. Plus, I've been pretty busy myself."

"With what?" she asks confused, her eyebrows scrunching together on her face.

"Well, after I turned down Fleming I quit my job. Yesterday was the end of my two weeks."

"So, now you're unemployed?" she asks, her smile replacing her frown.

"Unemployed but I am considering following in your footsteps and opening my own business. I have quite a few clients willing to follow me."

"That's great, Zack."

A few quiet moments pass, the sound of a ticking clock echoing through the space.

"Blake, what are we-,"

"I love you and I miss you. Can you forgive me for being an idiot? I promise that I'll reign in my temper."

Taking her in my arms I seal my lips against hers, taking delight in her taste, something I have missed in the last two weeks.

"I love you too. My life doesn't feel fulfilled without you in it."

Blake presses herself against me, and we spend the next hour christening the desk in her new office before we decide to head back to my house to spend the next few hours showing each other what we've missed.

"Mr. Fleming, I want to thank you for allowing me the chance to meet with you and your executives personally this morning." I listen to Blake inside the conference room as she delicately grovels to Fleming Coffee.

When she and I finally came up for air after a weekend in my bed, I explained to her what the opportunity that Fleming Coffee presents for her and her company. She called Thomas and he excitedly agreed to meet with her on Wednesday morning.

Blake was nervous this morning, but when we stepped out of the elevator on the sixth floor, she was transported back into her element.

"I'm sure many of you have been made aware of the situation that was presented to myself and a colleague regarding the terms to this contract."

A rustling of murmurs sound inside the room in agreement and I find myself smiling.

"Well, if you and your team are open to it, I have a new proposition for you all to consider."

"At the current point we are in, Ms. Holliday, I believe we are open to hearing what you have to say. We still stand behind our decision to support your campaign."

"Wonderful, I'm thrilled to hear it. Because I will only sign the contract if you're open to working with my new employee as well.

"Ladies and Gentlemen, I am thrilled to introduce you to Zack Nicholson, our newest member of BH Marketing."

I stroll into the conference room at my introduction to find Thomas standing from his chair with a warm grin on his face.

"Well, I can say that this is an interesting turn of events. It's good to see you, Mr. Nicholson."

Blake and I meet with the team for another few minutes to explain how the changes will affect the campaign; mainly that time spent will be split between Blake and me.

Joining her business was a no-brainer. I had been buried deep inside her sex when she spoke up with the idea. It was an easy decision and I agreed one hundred percent. Then we kept right on searching for our release.

We walk out of the building hand in hand with a ten-year contract to solidify her business for years to come.

"We did it," she whispers as we move toward my car.

"No, you did it. I just came along for the ride."

"I never would have imagined this if anyone had asked me ten years ago."

"Imagined what?"

"Us," she says, gazing up at me without a care in the world.

"What about the ruling the world part?"

"I'll get there one business at a time."

We stop in front of the car as I move to open her door.

"Hey, we were destined to happen at the right time, Blake. I wouldn't change anything about how we got to this moment."

"Even when I hated you?"

Cupping her chin in my hand, I tell her, "You never really hated me, but even then. I love you, beautiful."

Not giving her a chance to reply, I kiss her the way I should have all those years ago when I saw her sitting on that bench freshman year. A kiss that possesses us, dominates our bodies, and makes us one.

Whispering against my lips, Blake says, "Better late than never."

And truer words have never been spoken.

I WATCH AS BLAKE STANDS WITH HER FATHER and Maggie admiring the Eiffel Tower across the lawn from where we stand with a tour group.

Maggie and Mike are on their long-awaited vacation, the year almost up from when they could redeem the vacation package, while Blake and I are here on work.

Business has been booming. Our work with Fleming Coffee has started to gain a lot of notoriety in the community and we're here to meet with a globally recognized imprint company.

But today we get to play tourists while her father is in town with his new bride. Maggie and Mike eloped last month. Blake seemed surprised, but I wasn't. I saw it coming for a while.

My family's antique ring sparkles on Blake's finger as she takes a picture of the structure. She moved into my house once we made amends and after she convinced Thomas Fleming to take a chance on her company I had proposed.

I wish that I could say that the proposal was romantic and over the top, but it wasn't. We had been renovating the new workspace. Blake and I were covered in paint and woodchips but something inside me flipped and I needed to make her mine – now.

The ring I constantly kept in my pocket since she and I had gotten back together slipped easily into my palm. I spun around and kneeled before her, not even caring that my knee landed in a tray of paint and I poured my heart out. She cried and accepted, and I cried as I placed the ring on her finger.

But my man card stayed thoroughly intact because we fucked like rabbits for the next two days.

"Hey, babe. Want to see if my dad can take a picture of us?"

I'm brought back to the moment and walk over to Blake, wrapping my arms tightly around her waist.

"Are you bored?" she whispers, resting her chin on my chest looking up at me.

"Not at all. I'm enjoying watching you so happy."

"It's a magical place. I always dreamed of visiting. And here I am . . .with you." Blake places her hand on my cheek, the hand with her engagement ring shining brightly in the sun.

"I'm glad that I get to share this with you."

Her dad steps over to us and tells us to knock it off, but with a tender grin. It's taken him a while to warm up to me, but we're on good terms now. We've even gone out to grab a beer once he was able to walk freely from his wheelchair. When Blake and I got engaged, he became even more determined to walk again, wanting to have the chance to walk his daughter down the aisle.

"Do you think they'll notice if we sneak off?" I ask. The scent of her perfume tickling my senses shoots a spark of desire straight to my cock.

"What do you have in mind?" she questions saucily, rocking her hips against mine.

The crowd around us falls away; the awe of the structure across the lawn loses its luster. I'm solely focused on Blake.

"Think we can make it to the hotel room in fifteen minutes?"

Her eyes grow in excitement. "Is that a challenge?"

Egging her on as she bounces on her toes in anticipation, I say, "May the best person win." She bounces on her toes ready to launch herself toward the hotel but I toss her over my shoulder and carry her instead.

This is one challenge I have no intention of losing.

Stay in touch

Newsletter: http://bit.ly/2WokAjS
Author Page: www.facebook.com/authorreneeharless
Reader Group: http://bit.ly/31AGa3B
Instagram: www.instagram.com/renee_harless
Bookbub: www.bookbub.com/authors/renee-harless
Goodreads: http://bit.ly/2TDagOn
Amazon: http://bit.ly/2WsHhPq
Website: www.reneeharless.com

Acknowledgements

Firstly, I want to thank you, my reader! I'm so grateful every day for your love and support.

Thanks to my amazing team. Renee, Virginia, Amanda, Lisa, Shelly, Crystal, Paula, Sally, and Amanda. You keep me sane and I would be lost with you. Renee that you so much for everything that you do. I'm lucky to call you a friend and sister.

Thank you to the bloggers that have helped get the word out about this book, it means so much to me. Thank you to my ARC team for every message about your anticipation of this book. I'm honored to have you on my team.

To my family, my husband and two incredible children, thank you. There aren't enough words to express my gratitude at your patience and love and support through this process, especially when I'm just a few minutes late to dinner because I needed to finish up a chapter. I love you.

About the Author

Renee Harless is a romance writer with an affinity for wine and a passion for telling a good story.

Renee Harless, her husband, and children live in Blue Ridge Mountains of Virginia. She studied Communication, specifically Public Relations, at Radford University.

Growing up, Renee always found a way to pursue her creativity. It began by watching endless runs of White Christmas- yes even in the summer – and learning every word and dance from the movie. She could still sing "Sister Sister" if requested. In high school, she joined the show choir and a community theatre group, The Troubadours. After marrying the man of her dreams and moving from her hometown she sought out a different artistic outlet – writing.

To say that Renee is a romance addict would be an understatement. When she isn't chasing her kids around the house, working her day job, or writing, she jumps head first into a romance novel.